KAREN DAWN BLUM

KATE BAKER AND FRIENDS - VOLUME 2

SCHOOL STINKS!

KAREN DAWN BLUM

KAREN DAWN BLUM

COPYRIGHT

Summary: Middle School stinks. As if sixth grade wasn't bad enough, seventh grade is made more challenging when Kate Baker's arch enemy moves into her neighborhood and tries to steal her friends.

ISBN-13: 978-0692254592
ISBN-10: 0692254595

[1. Mystery 2. Middle School-Fiction 3. Friendship 4. Michigan-Fiction 5. Native American Folklore-Fiction 6. Horses-Riding 7. Detroit-Fiction 8. Academics 9.Canada-Fiction.]

DEDICATION

School Stinks! is dedicated to my brother, Daryl Michael Blum.

I will always remember him running, climbing, playing, and riding his bike painlessly, bravely and endlessly.

CONTENTS

SIGHT FOR SORE EYES

Seventh grade was starting in a few days. It was going to be my best year ever.

My school supplies were lined up on the desk in my room. My backpack was ready to be filled with books. I checked my list one last time.

"Mom, I have to go up to the corner. I need erasers. I'll be back in a while," I yelled as I left the house.

I walked out of our cul-de-sac and turned left. The drugstore was five blocks away. The Old Smith House was on the next intersection.

I always liked Mrs. Smith. When I was little, she paid me fifty cents an hour to pull weeds. Even when I accidentally pulled her 'prize petunias' she paid me in full.

There was a giant moving van on the street next to Mrs. Smith's house. As I walked toward the driveway I heard the creaky old screen door slam. Out of the door came a sight that made my eyes sore.

My life would never be the same.

CHAPTER I
HIT THE BOOKS

The man sitting across from us stared at me. I stared back at him. He looked away.

"They are practical. Black goes with everything. Look. Gym shoes are on sale. You buy one, you get one free! I can get a pair for my gym locker and one for home. That will save money and then we can afford the platform shoes. Please, please? Everyone will be wearing platforms. If I don't get them, I'll look like a baby in the seventh grade."

Mom took a long, deep breath, "Okay, you can get them, but you better wear them every day to school."

I glanced up to see if the man was still looking at me. He was gone.

"I'll wear them every day. Thanks so much. You are the best. I love you."

Our area of town was very hilly. That's why our middle schools were called West Hills and East Hills. I went to West Hills Middle School. My best friends from Temple, Susan and Emily, went to East Hills. In ninth grade we will finally all go to the same school, Lincoln High.

Last year, when I started sixth grade at West Hills I thought it was the biggest school in the world. I got lost the first few weeks. It didn't seem so big when I got used to it.

Seventh grade was going to be hard, but it

wasn't the classes or homework I was worried about. Facing The Cabbage again was going to be impossible.

Jo Ann, "The Cabbage", Elkavich, was my arch enemy at camp for three summers in a row. This past summer, she tricked me into thinking we were best friends. The first two weeks my old best friend at camp, Stacey, "The Pilgrim", Milgrim didn't show up and there was no choice but to become friends with that stinky traitor, The Cabbage.

I decided to stay two extra weeks at camp as a favor to her. Unexpectedly, The Pilgrim came to camp. That was when World War III broke out.

Of course, those two became best friends and banded against me. The rest is history. Two weeks dragged by and I was miserable.

I had to be friends with Shannon, "Little Miss Michigan Model", McClintock. All she ever talked about was her long, luxurious hair. After two weeks of agony at camp, I vowed I would never talk to The Cabbage again.

My bus stop was on the corner of Fairfax and Edison in front of the Old Smith House. Mrs. Smith let the kids wait in her foyer when the weather was bad. She served hot chocolate on cold days.

When I got back from camp, I walked by Mrs. Smith's house and found the Elkavich family moving in. The Cabbage would be living a total of six houses away, close enough for me to smell her.

When I walked to the corner store to buy my erasers, I took a different route so I would not pass by The Cabbage's house. There was no way I would be able to stay away from her on school days unless I came up with a plan to avoid going to the bus stop in front of her house.

I decided I would walk to school every day. I didn't think I would make it walking one and a half miles in my new platform shoes. I had to come up with a different plan.

On Labor Day, after we got home from the mall, I went online. I clicked on the link about bus routes to West Hills Middle School. Bus number 19 stopped in front of The Cabbage's house at 7:35 a.m. If I left my house a little early and pretended to go to that stop, I could walk half-a-mile up the hill on Baxter Avenue and cross over the highway on the Eton Street Bridge to catch bus number 24 at 7:42 a.m.

To be popular in the seventh grade, I had to look cool. I hung my new jeans with a short sleeve black t-shirt and my jean jacket on a hanger in my closet and took my new shoes out of the box so they were ready to slip into the next morning.

My hair was taking forever to grow. My mom thought short hair was easier to manage when I went to gymnastics. She didn't realize that cool girls had long hair. I figured by the time I had my Bat Mitzvah in one year, my hair would be to my waist.

On my way to bed, I went into my parents'

room. They were sitting in their chairs reading. I stepped over our dog, Seska, on my way through their room.

"Mom, can you drive me to school tomorrow?"

"No, Kathryn. I have to drive Timmy to school and get to work. Dr. Tyler needs me since the other hygienist is on maternity leave."

"You could drop me off on your way to work."

"Sorry. You have to go on the bus."

"Dad, can you drive me?"

"I have to be at the temple extra early to observe the Torah Study class," Dad answered.

Grown-ups were crazy. They didn't have to go to school, but they got up early and went to work to watch other people learn!

Tuesday morning, the first day of seventh grade, I put my lunch, a notebook for each class, and my planner into my backpack. So mom wouldn't see me walking to the other stop, I went toward The Cabbage's house, and cut through the Matthews' back yard and walked quickly up the hill and over the bridge to catch my new bus.

I got to the stop and stood in line with the other kids. When I climbed the steps into the bus, I kept my head down just in case. I didn't want the driver to notice I didn't belong on his bus.

Phew. He looked straight ahead. "Step to the rear of the bus. We have lots of kids to fit in here."

At school, we rushed to the gym for West Hills Middle School's first assembly of the year. The principal, vice principal and all the teachers were on the stage and the kids were crowded on the bleachers and sitting on the floor in rows on the basketball court. They still made us sit on the floor like we did in elementary school.

"Welcome back to school, students. We hope you had a great summer and are ready for a fun and exciting year of learning and working together. I will now turn over the microphone to Mrs. Brown, your Vice Principal, so she can go over the school rules with everyone." Principal Rodriguez didn't like to talk too much.

"Hello students. The seventh and eighth graders know me already. For you sixth graders, I am Mrs. Brown. You will not see me much unless you break the rules."

School was an endless list of rules and regulations. Didn't Mr. Rodriguez say we would have fun? All the rules didn't leave much chance for fun.

"We have six hundred students in this school. We have to maintain a safe and healthy environment to keep everyone in control.

You signed a behavioral contract before school started. You may refer to the contract guidelines if you have any questions. Just to sum it up so you can move on to your scheduled classes, I will remind you of the four major behaviors that will be expected of you.

Be courteous and be kind. Respect each other's space and respect each other's and the school's property. And students, one more thing. Last year there seemed to be a lack of respect for the dress code, so this year it will be adhered to more strictly," Mrs. Brown kept talking and talking.

Last year in sixth grade, my mom told me not to wear my new jeans until she had a chance to hem them with her sewing machine. I left the house one morning before she could notice I was wearing my too-long jeans to school.

When I was in Science class, Miss Tibble, the meanest teacher at West Hills, was walking around the classroom checking to see if we were doing our experiments correctly.

"Miss Baker."

I looked up and there she was, right in front of me. She had her hands on her hips.

"Yes, Miss Tibble. Am I doing my experiment right?"

"Miss Kate Baker. Report to the Vice Principal's office. It appears that your jeans are too long and do not conform to the West Hill's Middle School dress code."

"My pants aren't too long," I stood up and pulled my waist band as high as it would go.

"The hem is dragging on the floor. That is not allowed. Take a hall pass and go to Mrs. Brown's office at once," Miss Tibble said.

By then, everyone in the class had stopped working and was staring at me. I did not like to be the center of attention. I could feel my face getting redder and hotter by the minute. I grabbed the hall pass and walked to the Vice Principal's office.

"Miss Tibble sent me to see Mrs. Brown. I don't know what she has against me. I didn't do anything," I said under my breath as I sat in the chair by the door.

The secretary paged Mrs. Brown on her intercom. Within seconds she came out of her office and said, "Kate Baker, come right in."

"I don't know why Miss Tibble sent me here. I think she is just wasting your time, Mrs. Brown," I said in my sweetest voice.

"Kate. It looks like your jeans are too long and are touching the floor. That is not allowed according to the dress code. I could call your mother and have her bring you some shorter pants, or I could staple the hem up with my stapler. It is your choice," said Mrs. Brown.

"My mom will be so mad at you if you ruin my pants." Mom had told me not to wear those pants until she had a chance to hem them. I couldn't let Mrs. Brown win without a fight.

I walked out of the office with staples in my pant legs. It looked ridiculous. The kids in science class stared at my pants, but I acted like nothing had happened.

When I got home that day, I quickly used the staple remover and placed my pants on the mend pile next to mom's sewing machine. I didn't speak to Miss Tibble for the rest of the sixth grade.

I looked at my shoes. They were so cool. There was nothing in the dress code saying platforms were not allowed. My pants were not too long.

They were about one inch from the floor when I stood up.

The bell was ringing. Mrs. Brown was done with her speech about the school rules. It was time to start the seventh grade.

I walked to my first class. Math was not my favorite, but it wasn't my least favorite, either. Mr. Kulis had everyone sit in their assigned seats.

He talked about what we would do all year. There was going to be a boat-load of homework, quizzes and tests in algebra.

"I will call each of you up in alphabetical order. Grab a book and I'll record the number in my record book. Since these books are brand new, the school board expects that no marks will be put into any of your textbooks," said Mr. Kulis.

He had us write our homework assignment in our planners. I hoisted the textbook into my arms along with my notebooks and went off to my next class. We got a heavy textbook and a homework assignment from every teacher. We even had a textbook for gym class.

Thank goodness The Cabbage was only in Social Studies with me last hour. I didn't look at her once. I noticed her staring at my new shoes. She wasn't wearing platforms. She was wearing flats. She wasn't very stylish.

There were 200 kids in each grade at West Hills Middle School. There were 75 from my elementary, Edison, and the other 125 came from the bigger elementary school, Hamilton. When classes were changing, you had to fight your way through masses of kids hurrying to their lockers.

Between classes, we seventh graders stopped at our lockers on the second floor to get books or lunches. By the time I went to my locker at the end of the first day, I could barely fit all the books into my backpack. It was so heavy that when I finally got it on my back, I thought I was going to fall over.

I trudged toward bus number 24. I knew it would be hard to walk the long way home from the bus stop across the bridge, but at least it was downhill most of the way. It was worth it not to have to ride on the same bus as The Cabbage.

The elementary kids walked home, but mom liked picking Timmy up from school on the days she didn't work or got off work early. When she worked, Timmy would be walking home by himself Since I got my Red Cross Babysitting Certificate last spring, I would be watching him until Mom got home from work.

Besides going to regular school five days a week, I had a very busy after school and weekend schedule. Monday Night School would start at the temple next week. I went to gymnastics on Tuesdays and Thursdays. On Friday night and Saturday morning I went to services for Shabbat. I used to go to Sunday school at the temple, but now that my Bat Mitzvah was in one year, I would be starting Mitzvah Club on Wednesdays after school.

No one was home when I got there after my

first day of seventh grade. I ate a quick snack and started my homework.

My backpack was so heavy I was probably going to end up with a hernia or a slipped disc. I didn't know what either one of those things were, but I had heard my grandma talking about them with her sisters on the phone while she was here when I got back from camp. She had gone back to her house in Canada one week before school started, right after my birthday.

"It was so nice to spend time with you, Kate. I hope you have a great school year. Please try to be friends with Jo Ann again. You have so much in common and now she only lives a few houses away. How lucky you are to have someone your own age so near," Grandma said.

"Thanks Grandma. I had fun with you, too. Now you better get in the car and go to the airport. Dad is waiting for you." Grandma left, but I would be seeing her again in the summer.

"Hi, Kate we're home. How was your first day?" asked my mom as she and Timmy came in the door.

"It was great. I have tons of homework." I walked toward my bedroom.

"I had the best day. Fourth grade is awesome. All my friends are in my class. I have the best teacher and this Friday I get to bring home the class guinea pig," Timmy said as he followed me into my room.

"Did you tell the teacher that Seska ate Shelly,

our turtle? I bet she won't let you bring home the class guinea pig when she finds out," I said.

When I was in the second grade, we rescued a German shepard dog named Seska from the Humane Society. Right after we got the dog we couldn't find our turtle. Shelly never left his bowl. We didn't see her do it, but we were pretty sure the dog ate our turtle.

"Seska doesn't bother Izzy and Lizzy. And she hasn't eaten Allie, yet," Timmy replied.

"It is a good thing that Izzy and Lizzy are vegetarians. They won't eat the guinea pig, but Allie or Seska might!"

"Oh Kate, Allie won't eat the class guinea pig, will she?" Timmy asked.

"I'm just kidding. Get out of my room. You are not allowed in here." I had to be careful not to be too nice to Timmy. When I let him into my room he touched everything and moved my things around.

Timmy ran down to the kitchen for his after school snack. I heard him go down to the family room to see our pet iguanas, Lizzy and Izzy. They had the run of the house. They came upstairs to wait by the fridge while my mom got their dinner ready.

Two years before, my dad went to Florida to visit his mom and dad, my Bubby and Zadye. He came back with a baby alligator and two baby green iguanas.

When we first got Lizzy and Izzy, they were

about one foot long from the tip of their nose to the end of their tail. Now they were three feet long, about half the length they would be when full-grown.

Seska never bothered the iguanas. She was pretty scared of them. Allie lived in Mom and Dad's room in the turtle bowl on top of their dresser where Seska couldn't reach.

Allie the alligator hadn't grown as much as Lizzy and Izzy. She was about fifteen inches long. We didn't know if she was a she, but the name sounded good, so we called her a girl. When it felt cool in her room, Mom would put Allie in her housecoat pocket to keep her warm.

When people came over, they freaked out. It wasn't every day that you saw a family with two huge iguanas living free in the family room. They had a huge plastic palm tree to climb on and they lounged on the window sill when the sun was shining. The alligator in my mom's pocket was more peculiar to some people.

I got back to my homework. I needed to get organized before I could study. I had eight classes and the books were stacked up on my desk. I was sure going to have a backache carrying them to school every day.

I went through my class requirements for the year. After algebra first hour, I had elective period. This semester I had art, next semester I would have Choir with Mr. Balbes.

My art teacher, Mrs. Saslove, dressed so cool.

She owned an art gallery in the mall. Our first project was going to be jewelry design.

My third hour class, skills for living, was required for all seventh graders. It was divided up into four units of study that we would rotate through in nine-week segments.

The shop segment included conservation and home safety. We would be learning how to use power tools and make a project out of wood. The cooking segment focused on dietetics and eating to stay healthy.

The first lesson in the sewing segment would be fashion history. I could totally understand teaching boys how to keep themselves clean and how to wash their clothes, but why would they sit through the history of fashion? In sewing, I was planning to make a pair of pajama bottoms. Mom already took me to the fabric store to pick out some cool fleece material with a horse design.

In the personal safety segment, the last nine weeks of school, we would learn CPR and first aid. Then we would be learning about the "facts of life" with boys in the room!

In fifth grade the boys and girls were separated for one class period. Our moms came in to be with us. We talked about puberty and menstruation. I still don't know what the boys talked about.

Steven Lancaster, the cutest, most popular boy at West Hills, was in my skills for living class. Hopefully no one would find out that our moms had us take baths together when we were toddlers.

At least I wouldn't have to put up with that possible embarrassment until the end of the seventh grade.

Science with Miss Tibble was my fourth hour class. It was bad enough having her for a teacher in sixth grade. How would I put up with her again?

It was going to be hard to wait to eat lunch until after four hours of classes. I was going to have to bring a snack to eat between art and skills for living. I was hoping to have some friends in my lunch hour. The Cabbage had the nerve to try to sit at my lunch table today! I told her to find somewhere else to sit.

After lunch, I had fifth-hour language arts with Mr. Spangler.

"Be prepared, students. There will be many writing assignments and you will learn to use proper grammar this year," Mr. Spangler was going to give us so much homework. I was never going to have any free time.

Sixth hour was our split class. Everyone had to take physical education and foreign language. First semester I would go to gym three days a week and foreign language two days a week. Second semester I would go to foreign language three days and gym two days.

I hated gym. I always got chosen last for teams. After sweating for an hour, I wished gym was at the end of the day so I wouldn't have to risk having B.O. during school.

I got the best grades in Spanish last year, and

decided it was easier than Mandarin Chinese or French. I got the best teacher, Mrs. Mandelbaum, for Spanish this year.

If you did well in your foreign language, during spring break of eighth grade, you could go on a trip to China, Spain or France. You had to sell things to help raise money for the trip and your parents make up the difference. I had no doubt I could sell enough wrapping paper, candy bars and magazine subscriptions to all of Mom and Dad's friends and our relatives so I will go to Spain next year.

Social studies with Miss Jenkins, my favorite teacher, would be my last class of the day. Last year in her class we did plays about our favorite historical characters. Miss Jenkins had local businesses donate prizes. Our group won gift cards from Walmart. I used mine to buy a docking station for my digital music player.

Miss Jenkins would be announcing the teams in November for our big Make a Difference term project that would take most of the school year and be due in May. I wanted to win so I could get another prize.

I memorized my schedule and avoided The Cabbage the first week of school. The second week had begun and mom dropped me off at the temple for the first Monday Night School of the year. My dad was already at the temple. I stopped in his office to see him.

"Hi, Flo. Is my dad in his office?"

"He is in there with Rabbi. You want to wait,

Doll?" My dad's secretary Flo knew me since I was a baby. She was a sweet lady, but when you got sent to the principal's office for doing something wrong in the religious school, watch out, Flo was not so sweet!

"No, I'll go to the social hall and wait for dinner. I'm hungry."

"Okay, Doll. I'll tell your dad you stopped in."

There were twenty large round tables set up in the dining hall. Each class had about thirty students. Kids from all over attended Monday Night School, even if they weren't members of the temple.

Emily, Susan and I Face Timed on Sunday Night. They asked me to save seats for them. I sat at one of the tables for seventh graders.

"Those shoes are so cool, Kate," said Emily.

"Em. I love your jeans. You look nice, too, Susan," I said.

This was going to be a great year.

"Hi. Can I sit here?" Elliot Einstein asked pointing to an empty seat at our table.

"It is taken. You better sit somewhere else," I said as he walked away.

"It looks like Elliot has a crush on you, Kate," said Susan.

"Why didn't you let him sit there?" asked Emily.

There was no way I would let a nerd like him sit with us. He would be talking about bugs and other weird scientific stuff.

"I can't let him sit with us. My boyfriend, Steven Lancaster, will get jealous."

"You didn't tell us you have a boyfriend. Who is he, Kate?" Emily asked.

"You know, he's the hottest boy at my school."

Since Susan and Emily didn't go to West Hills, they would never learn that Steven didn't know I existed.

By the end of the school year, I was planning to have Steven Lancaster as my *real* boyfriend.

I saw Elliot looking over at us. Why did he follow me around like a puppy dog? This crush he has had on me since we were in nursery school would never end. Why did he find me so irresistible?

Elliot would have to settle for being my lab partner in Miss Tibble's science class.

CHAPTER 2
HOWLING FOR HALLOWEEN

Fall had arrived. It was cool in the mornings and the leaves were changing colors. Walking to the far bus stop was a chore. My backpack was very heavy and while wearing my platform shoes, I needed to walk the least amount possible.

That day, besides all my other books, I had to bring my social studies book. There was no room for my lunch bag so I hung it from the strap of my backpack. As I walked I felt the lunch bag thump against my right leg.

I thought about going to the closer bus stop, but there was no way I would ever wait for the bus in front of The Cabbage's house. As I walked up the big hill, I leaned forward to keep from toppling over backward. I learned that trick from riding horses.

It sounded like a bus was coming up the hill behind me and I turned to see if it was my bus. Good. It wasn't a bus. It was a moving van. Oh, no! I lost my balance, and felt myself fall backwards. Before I knew it, I hit the ground. I was laying on my back on top of my backpack.

I felt like an upside down turtle, on top of her shell. I was flailing my legs and arms, trying to roll over on my side. I needed to get the backpack off my back in order to stand up again.

I felt something under my leg. My lunch was squished. Great! I was going to have to buy lunch.

I hated school lunches. The only thing more disgusting than school lunch was camp food.

I kept flailing my arms and trying to roll over so I could stand up. I heard a loud roaring sound. I looked up to see a bus thundering down the road. The kids were sticking their heads out of the windows, laughing at me.

I strained my head to see what bus it was as it drove away. Since I was lying on the ground, the number was upside-down. It was bus number 24. Hopefully no one recognized me.

I had officially missed my bus.

As I lay there a few cars drove by. I wished one of them would stop to help me, but I didn't want to see anyone I knew.

I yelled, hoping someone in the house I was laying in front of would hear me and rescue me. Unfortunately, most of the people in our neighborhood worked during the day.

I heard a car slow down and stop. The car door opened. A shadow came over me and blocked the sun. I looked up. It was Aubra, the Cabbage's older sister.

"What did you do now? You are a weird kid, Kate. You look like an upside-down turtle laying there."

"Don't be funny, Aubra. Can you help me up?"

"C'mon," Aubra said as she grabbed my hand.

"Why are you not in school?" I asked.

"I went to the dentist."

That was funny; my mom didn't tell me Aubra

had an appointment.

"Why are you on this side of the highway?" Aubra asked.

"I missed the bus."

Aubra looked me in the eye. I looked her in the eye. We both could see the other wasn't telling the truth.

"I didn't go to the dentist. I skipped school," Aubra admitted.

"I didn't miss the bus, I was avoiding your sister."

"Promise you won't tell?" asked Aubra.

"I won't tell if you don't tell."

"Pinky swear?"

We locked pinkies.

"Will you please drive me?'

"Okay. Get in the car," Aubra said as she loaded my backpack into the back seat. "Man! That's a heavy bag. What do you have in there? Rocks?"

"No rocks. A ton of books. It seems heavier every day. I can't let anyone find out what happened."

"I won't tell anyone."

"If we hurry I won't be late to school. This would be hard to explain," I said.

"You don't know what it's like to start at a new school. You have always lived in the same neighborhood. It's hard to fit in when you're new. I miss my old friends."

I couldn't believe someone as cool as Aubra had a hard time making friends.

I felt important as I quietly listened to Aubra talk. While she was talking, I came up with a bright idea.

"Aubra, our temple has a 'Bring a Friend' to Monday Night School program. I can bring you! There are lots of cool kids in your grade. Would you like to come with me next Monday?"

"Wow that sounds great. I'll meet you there."

Aubra dropped me off at school. The buses were in the driveway and kids were still walking into the building. I was putting my coat and my squished lunch in my locker when The Cabbage walked up.

"I saw Aubra drop you off. Why did my sister drive you to school?"

"That's none of your business."

"Wow, Kate. You are so mean. I'll find out. I'll ask my mom," she said.

"No, don't ask your mom." I didn't want Aubra to get into trouble. "Aubra had a dentist appointment and she saw me walking to the bus and offered to drive me," I fibbed.

"We went to the dentist last week, Kate. Your mom cleaned our teeth. I hope my sister isn't skipping school again. Mom will kill her," said The Cabbage.

I didn't think Aubra would tell on me, and I promised her I wouldn't tell on her. I didn't know what to say to The Cabbage, so I ignored her, turned around, and went into the girl's lavatory before algebra class.

When I was in kindergarten, I thought the teacher was asking us, "Children, do you have to go to the laboratory? I thought, "Do I have to do an experiment? Is there a scientist in there?" It took me a while to realize she meant the bathroom.

In kindergarten, the lavatories were in the back of the classroom. I noticed that they smelled very bad. I avoided them as much as possible. I tried to limit my bathroom visits to peeing and tried to hold on until I got home if I had to poop. When I did have to use the bathroom at school, I plugged my nose and ran in and out as fast as possible.

Our kindergarten teacher read us a book, and after that, I was having so much fun coloring, I ignored my stomach messaging me that I had to poop. It was my turn to be student of the week. I didn't want to miss my favorite snack that day. My mom sent animal cracker boxes with the carrying string for each of the kids in my class.

Since I brought the snack, I got to pass out the milk and cookie boxes. Before we were allowed to eat, the teacher told us to use the lavatory and wash our hands. I ran in and washed my hands.

By the time snack was over, my stomach was killing me. To this day, I remember the pain. As I ran to the bathroom, poop started coming out of me. I didn't make it to the toilet.

I stayed in the lavatory. I didn't want anyone to know I had pooped my pants. I thought, only babies pooped their pants. My brother, Timmy was a baby. He wore diapers. I had been wearing panties since I was three. After what seemed like an eternity, two girls came into the lavatory.

"Ooh, it smells like someone pooped their pants," said the class know-it-all, Mallory.

"Kate, did you poop your pants?" asked Mallory's best friend, Kelsey. They were inseparable.

"I didn't poop my pants. Someone's dog came in here and pooped on the floor. I am cleaning it up."

"We're telling the teacher on you, Kate Baker," they said as they ran out of the bathroom.

I was horrified. The teacher came into the bathroom. She wasn't plugging her nose, and it stunk in there.

"Kate, are you okay? Did you have an accident? Go into the bathroom stall and I will help clean you up," the teacher said as she pulled on some rubber gloves and got a box of baby wipes out of the cabinet in the corner. The teacher proceeded to clean up my bum. I cried the whole time. I was humiliated.

"Don't worry, Kate. Children have accidents. It seems they don't want to go to the bathroom when they are having fun. Please go right away next time. The fun will still be there when you return," she said as she got a spare pair of panties and jeans out of the cabinet. "These look like they will fit you just fine." My Kindergarten teacher was so sweet. Too bad the teachers got meaner as the students got older.

I washed my hands and face and I was happy again when I came out of the bathroom.

"Hey Poopy-Pants. Are those boy's jeans you are wearing?" asked Kelsey.

I knew a dog didn't go into the bathroom," said Mallory. The rest of the class heard them and laughed at me.

That morning, before my first class, I went into the West Hills' girls' lavatory and unfortunately, Mallory and Kelsey were standing in front of the sinks looking at themselves in the mirror. I hated being around Mallory and Kelsey, especially in the bathroom. I didn't know if they remembered the Kindergarten Incident, but I didn't want to remind them of it.

I ignored them. I went into the stall and put some toilet paper on the floor and my backpack on top to keep it from getting germs. After I peed, I waited a few minutes until I heard Mallory and Kelsey leave. I used my foot to flush and went out of the stall.

I made it to algebra just in time. The day started out bad with me falling over like a turtle. Then I saw the mean girls, Mallory and Kelsey. I hoped The Cabbage would keep her big mouth shut so Aubra and I wouldn't get into trouble.

The next Monday night I got to the temple early. I went into the social hall to eat dinner. Aubra was standing by the high school tables.

"My sister came with me," Aubra said. "She wants to join Monday Night School, too."

Oh, my, gosh! Me and my big mouth. Why on earth did I invite Aubra? Couldn't she leave her stinky sister at home? The Cabbage was invading my territory. I was going to have to see her at Monday Night School and at regular school.

The Cabbage was already sitting at my regular table. She was talking to Emily and Susan. Elliot Einstein was sitting next to The Cabbage.

I sat down next to Emily. There wasn't much I could do to change this situation. I had to put up with the seating arrangement or risk losing my two best friends at the temple.

Two days later, on Wednesday, I had just arrived home from Mitzvah Club. I was in my room doing homework. My Torah portion was very difficult. Genesis was the longest and most confusing of all the parts you could be assigned.

"Why was the world created? Why did God want Adam to have a wife?" The instructor, Mr. Levine, always ended a sentence with a question. Luckily I had eleven months to find out the answers.

"Kate, you have a phone call," mom yelled from the kitchen.

"Okay, mom, I'll get the phone up here," I called back.

"Hello, this is Kate," I said.

"Hi, Kate, this is Jessica Cohen. I got your number from the babysitting list in the Temple Bulletin. I have two sons and I need a regular sitter on Saturday nights. Would you be able to come this Saturday to meet the boys and sit for a couple hours?" she asked.

I had been wondering if anyone would ever call. My ad was in the bulletin for two months already. When I first took the Red Cross Babysitting class last spring, I was only eleven.

I had to be a mother's helper before I could babysit alone. I helped our neighbor, Mrs. Collins, with her baby, Cassidy. She was so sweet. After a few times, Mr. and Mrs. Collins went out with another couple for dinner. I was nervous and my mom promised to come over if I needed her as back-up.

Cassidy was asleep when I walked over. Her mom and dad left the baby monitor turned on. They said they'd be home in one hour and a half, after dinner.

There was a pan of brownies, fresh out of the oven, on the stove.

"Kate, you are welcome to have a brownie if you'd like a snack while we're gone," said Mrs. Collins. She was so nice.

I checked the baby monitor. There wasn't a peep from Cassidy. I was bored, so I ate a brownie.

My mom texted me, "Kate how is the baby?"

I texted back, "She is sleeping."

"Okay. Keep up the good work and call if you need me," Mom texted.

I did some homework. I was bored again, so I ate another brownie. By the time the Collins came home, I had eaten all but one brownie.

They brought another couple home with them.

"Where are the brownies?" Mrs. Collins asked. "I was planning on serving them to our friends."

"I am sorry. I didn't know," I explained.

Mrs. Collins paid me. I didn't feel great about taking the money. She never called me again. I decided that the next time I babysat I would ask if there was any food I couldn't eat.

Mrs. Cohen was waiting for an answer.

"I would love to sit for your boys. What time do you want me to come?"

"Since it is the first time, I will pick you up at six o'clock, bring you over to review the emergency sheet and show you around our house. The other Saturdays we'll need you to sit from around six until eleven. Is that okay, Kate?" Mrs. Cohen sounded nice, but a little desperate.

"Okay. I'll see you at six on Saturday," I said.

Saturday couldn't come soon enough. I was going to need money to go to the mall and the movies. I figured babysitting for two little boys would be easy since I had a lot of practice babysitting for my little brother, Timmy.

At ten before six, Mrs. Cohen showed up in front of my house and blew the horn. I grabbed my coat and my backpack and ran out to her car.

"Hi, Kate," said Mrs. Cohen. She looked at my backpack. "I don't think you'll have time to do homework tonight. We won't be gone long. We're going for a quick bite."

"I didn't bring homework. I brought crafts to

do with the boys," I said.

At my Red Cross Babysitting course, we learned that busy kids equal happy kids.

"Here we are. Let's hurry, Mr. Cohen doesn't like to eat too late," said Mrs. Cohen.

We went into her house. There were toys scattered everywhere from wall-to-wall. My mom would not approve. Everything at our house was neat and organized.

Mr. Cohen yelled, "Boys, please come down right now, your sitter is here."

I heard a loud crash coming from upstairs. Two blond-haired, blue-eyed boys came bounding into the kitchen.

"Kate these are the twins, Bryan and Ryan. They're four years old."

"Four and a half, mom," said one of the boys. "We are identical twins," said the other.

I wasn't sure who was who!

"Hi, I'm Kate. I brought some fun crafts for us to do while your mom and dad are out to dinner," I said.

"Yeah, we are going to do crafts," Bryan and Ryan yelled as they jumped up and down.

"The boys have eaten dinner. There is a snack on the counter for you and the twins," said Mrs. Cohen, answering my next question and saving me future embarrassment at the same time.

After Mrs. Cohen showed me around and went over the rules and emergency plans, she and Mr. Cohen left for dinner. I still couldn't tell them apart, but the boys were cute and seemed well-behaved. This babysitting job would be easy money and maybe even a little fun.

The week before Halloween, Mom called Timmy and I into the kitchen. Izzy and Lizzy were standing in front of the fridge waiting for their dinner.

"I have great news. First Kate, could you please take this dish down to the lower level for the iguanas?" asked Mom.

I took the dish of vegetables down the stairs, "C'mon guys, time to eat," I said as Iz and Liz followed me down to the lower level. I set their food by the plastic palm tree and I ran up the stairs to find out what the great news was.

"I got an e-mail from the Forresters. There's going to be a Harvest Party at Camp Anishinabe next Sunday. It will be a blast. We're going to leave early in the morning. Timmy, you get to miss Sunday School! Dad can't get off so we'll be driving up with the Diane and her girls," my mom, the expert planner, said.

"I get to miss Sunday school and go to camp. I can't wait. I hope all my friends will be there."

Timmy was so goofy. I couldn't understand why he loved that awful camp. It was full of bugs, and they didn't have real bathrooms. You had to use an outhouse. Yuck.

"There is no way I am going anywhere with Jo Ann. It's bad enough that you made me go to camp four summers in a row. It will be torture going there during the school year. You told me I never had to go back. I hate Camp Anishinabe."

"Kathryn. Please don't raise your voice to me. The plans are already made and I responded to the invitation for us three. It will be fun. We are going to the Harvest Party and that is final," Mom said.

All week I tried to come up with excuses not to go to Camp Anishinabe. I walked outside with wet hair, trying to catch a cold. Nothing happened, not even a sniffle. I called Mrs. Cohen to ask if I could babysit for free. She didn't need me. I told Mom I had super bad cramps. Mom told me to take some ibuprofen.

On that dreaded Sunday morning, The Cabbage, Aubra and their mom drove up our driveway and tooted their horn. I sat way in the back of their mini-van with Timmy. No way was I going to sit next to The Cabbage.

I was quiet during the entire trip. Mom could make me go with them, but she couldn't make me talk.

Mrs. Elkavich and my mom met at Camp Anishinabe when they were girls. They were in the front seat singing camp songs and telling stories from their days at camp. We arrived after one of the longest rides of my life.

The huge banner hanging over the front of the main lodge read, 'Welcome Back to Camp Anishinabe. See How We Have Changed.'

Nothing would change my mind about that

horrible camp!

"Hi Sis. Aubra and Jo Ann, I swear you girls have grown in two months! I missed you so much," said Sharon Forrester as she hugged The Cabbage, her mom and her sister. The Cabbage's family was related to the owners of the camp. That was why she and Aubra got special treatment.

Sharon hugged my mom, Timmy and me. "Hi guys. It's so nice to see you. We have many activities planned today. Before the other camp families arrive, I want to give you guys the grand tour. We've made a lot of changes. You're going to love it."

I looked around. It had only been two months since camp ended and already it was different. There was a new cabin behind the main lodge. A sign on the door read, 'The Forresters Will Live Here.' Next to that was a first aid cabin with a huge red cross painted on the door.

My mouth must have been hanging open in shock, because Tom Forrester came up and said, "Kate. You look surprised. I told you we were going to improve the camp. We even have boys' and girls' bathrooms attached to the main lodge!"

We walked over to the new cabins. Although not quite finished, there were going to be flushing toilets and showers and huge bedrooms for each age group. They were even planning to have real bunk-beds.

"Kate, we will be removing it soon, but you can use the outhouse today if you need to," Tom said.

"Me use the outhouse? You must be joking."

Everyone laughed.

"Hey, what about us boys? Are we going to have cool cabins like the girls?"

"Yes, Timmy. We will start building the boys' cabins next week. You guys won't have to walk all the way across camp to use the outhouse. You'll have your own bathrooms in your cabins, too." said Tom.

Timmy, with his short attention span, saw the Forrester's kids on the play field and ran to meet them.

The new buildings were impressive, but it didn't make me want to come back to Camp Anishinabe. I suffered way too much with the nasty Cabbage and her friend, Stacey, The Pilgrim, Milgrim. It was settled. I was going to Camp Ticonderoga with Susan and Emily next summer.

We walked toward the play field. Many former campers and their families were arriving. The only person I wanted to see was Nick Caputo. He was the cutest boy at camp.

The families at the harvest party picked up their schedules for the day as they checked in at the main lodge. Our family was paired up with the Elkavich family. It figured. A day off from school and I had to spend it with The Cabbage.

The first activity was a sack race. I could see more families checking in. Two girls with blonde hair came toward me.

"Mandi and Amanda, wow, you look different! I

mean, you aren't dressed the same anymore."

"Hi, Kate. I decided to get my hair cut shorter," said Amanda.

"Yes. And we aren't wearing matching clothes" said Mandi.

They didn't talk at the same time nor did they finish each other's sentences!

"How did the last session at camp go when we left, Kate?" asked Amanda.

"It was horrible. Jo Ann stole my best friend, Stacey, and they wouldn't include me in anything."

"You know that isn't true," said The Cabbage.

She snuck up and interrupted my conversation.

"You are still a buttinsky," I said. "Go away. We weren't talking to you."

She didn't move.

"Hi Jo Ann. How've you been?" asked Mandi.

"I am great. Since you girls are late, would you like me to take you on a tour of the new cabins?" The Cabbage asked.

She left with the twins. Good riddance. Who needs them, anyway? They were never my friends.

I walked over to the group waiting to start the sack races. Even though he had his back to me, I recognized Nick Caputo.

"Kate. I can't believe you are here. I didn't get to say good-bye to you when camp ended last summer. Maybe today we'll have a chance to dance?" Nick asked.

I was about to answer him. My mouth went dry. I started coughing. Sharon blew the whistle to get everyone's attention. Nick ran toward his family.

The twins and The Cabbage stayed together for the sack race. I teamed up with Aubra. We each put one leg into the sack. We started hopping. We were almost to the finish line. Aubra was faster than me and it was hard to keep up with her. I fell over and caused us to lose the race.

"That's okay, Kate. I didn't care if we won. We will do better next time," said Aubra. She was being very nice to me since she saved me from being an upside down turtle. She probably was afraid I would tell on her for skipping school. She should have been more worried about her stinky sister telling on her than me.

After the activities in the play field, it was time to have lunch in the main lodge. I figured the sooner we finished lunch, the sooner this day would be over and we could drive back home and I could get away from Jo Ann.

Everyone stood behind the benches and we sang the Camp Anishinabe Song and the blessing in a round. It amazed me that most of the parents knew the words. They must have gone to Camp Anishinabe like my mom.

Camp Anishinabe Song

On the waters of Lake Hayanu

With the clear blue skies above,

There's a place we come together

It's a happy place we love.
Camp Anishinabe
All summer we are here,
With songs and games and friends
We'll be back here next year.

Camp Anishinabe Blessing
All Day long we work and play
And now it's time to pray.
God Bless us all
With health and strength,
And thank you for this food.
Amen.

The Forresters must have been trying to impress the parents. The food actually looked appetizing and tasted good.

The Cabbage was sitting at the table with the twins and Nick Caputo's family. That wasn't fair. How did she get to sit with them and I was stuck with my mom and Timmy? Timmy's friend, Billy, was at our table with his family.

Everyone laughed when Tom, the camp director said, "folks. lunch is over and since there is no mail call, we'll go down to the stable and start our hayride."

We left the main lodge and walked toward the

corral. Mandi came running toward me.

"Kate, come with us. We want to get on the same hay wagon with you," she said.

"No that's okay. I'll stay with my mom."

We gathered at the entrance to the stable. The wagons were hitched up to horses and lined up around the corral fence. Happy, my favorite horse, wasn't anywhere to be seen.

"These horses are Clydesdales. They are special, strong workhorses. We borrowed them for the day from the farm down the road. Our riding horses are being taken care of by camper's families for the winter. These families have kindly agreed to board them near their homes and take care of them until next summer," Tom explained.

"Our niece, Jo Ann, one of the stable-hands during camp, has agreed to take care of King, our prize stallion," Tom finished. Everyone was applauding.

It was just like The Cabbage to steal the attention. She was so lucky. She got special treatment during camp by being the niece of the owners, and now she got to have a horse.

I couldn't stand her. I was glad I didn't have to go on same hay wagon with her. We rode around in the itchy hay for a long time. My legs were falling asleep and I started sneezing. My eyes were itchy and my nose was running when the ride was finally over.

We walked back to the main lodge. Cider and donuts were set up on picnic tables. Skip, one of the camp counselors was at the DJ stand spinning the tunes. Right away, people started dancing.

"C'mon Kate. Let's dance," said my mom as she grabbed my hand and pulled me into the crowded dance area. "What's wrong, darling?" Mom asked. "It looks like you are crying."

"I'm not crying I am having an allergic reaction to the hay in the wagon," I said.

I looked over at Nick Caputo. He was dancing with that traitor, The Cabbage. She stole Stacey, The Pilgrim, from me at camp, and now she stole Nick Caputo from me. The worst part was, she lived six houses away from me and was trying to get in my group at Monday Night School. And she had a horse! I noticed the water in my eyes had turned to tears.

"Mom, I have to go to the bathroom," I said as I quickly walked away from the dance and toward the Elkavich's van. I was not going to participate in anymore camp activities. I was done with Camp Anishinabe.

When we were driving away from the camp I pretended to be asleep so I didn't have to talk to anyone. The last thing I thought I heard as I really drifted off to sleep was Timmy saying, "Kate will go trick-or-treating with you, Jo Ann. She knows all the best houses with the best candy." It had to be my imagination. Otherwise it was my worst nightmare ever.

At school on Halloween, The Cabbage approached me in the lunch room.

"What are you dressing up as tonight, Kate? What time should I come to your house?" The Cabbage asked.

Did she really think I was going trick-or-treating with her?

"I don't plan my costume like a little kid. I find something to wear at the last minute, besides, I never asked you to come with me," I answered.

The Cabbage turned around to walk away. I could tell she looked sad. No one deserved to miss Halloween candy.

"Be at my house at six-thirty," I said.

"Okay, see you then," The Cabbage smiled.

Since it was Thursday, I had gymnastics after school. My mom was waiting for me in her car at the parent's door.

"I heard you invited Jo Ann to go out begging with you. That was very nice of you," said my mom.

"How do you know that already? Did she send out smoke signals?"

"That is not nice, Kate. You shouldn't say things like that. In fact, Jo Ann texted her mom and her mom called me. She was so happy. It has been very difficult for Jo Ann to make friends since they moved here."

"Just because she is going out with me for Halloween doesn't mean we are friends."

The sun was setting and it was time to go trick-or-treating. I was wearing the Native American dress my mom made me for camp and the feathered head dress The Cabbage gave me at the final powwow at camp last summer.

When the doorbell rang, I was in the kitchen with my map of the neighborhood spread out on the table. I had all of the best houses marked with scary skeleton stickers. I was planning a strategy that would fill my king-size pillowcase with the most candy.

"Hi, Kate. I'm ready." I looked up. The Cabbage was wearing her authentic Native American dress and her head dress.

"What were you thinking? I don't want to go out with you and have people think we are twins. You have to change," I said.

"I am not changing. It is a coincidence. I didn't know what you were wearing. We look great. We could win a Halloween costume contest."

Timmy came into the kitchen wearing his Batman costume. "Get the Batmobile gassed up, Alfred!" Timmy laughed at his dumb joke

"Mom, why do I have to take Timmy? He is so annoying."

"Kate. If you don't want to take Timmy, you can stay home and Dad will take him. Stop being mean," Mom said.

"Wait a minute," I said.

I ran upstairs and got another king-size pillow case out of the linen closet. I threw it to The Cabbage.

"You will need this," I said as she caught the pillow case. "Okay. Let's go."

I didn't want to ruin Halloween. This was the only time of year my mom let us have candy. She made us give half away to poor kids, but keeping half was better than none.

We followed my plan and went to the houses that gave the best candy in the previous years. The later it got, the fuller my bag got. When my pillow case was busting at the seams, and almost too heavy to carry, we headed for home.

We sat in the middle of the family room floor and dumped out our bags of candy.

"Oh my gosh! What is that?" screamed The Cabbage as Lizzy lumbered over and sat next to her.

"That's Lizzy, our iguana. She won't hurt you." I had never seen The Cabbage afraid of anything.

"Are there any more surprises?" she asked.

"Izzy is here somewhere, too. They won't hurt you, they're curious. We have an alligator upstairs in my parents' room, too."

"Yeah, and our dog ate our turtle," said Timmy.

We finished sorting our candy. It was getting late. I still had some homework to finish before bed.

The doorbell rang.

"Kate, Aubra is here to walk Jo Ann home. Can you send her up?" Dad called down from upstairs.

"Well, I guess I better get home. Thanks for letting me go trick-or-treating with you," said the Cabbage." I'll see you at the bus stop tomorrow."

No way was I going on the same bus as her.

CHAPTER 3
MAKE A WISH-BONE

Halloween turned out to be so much fun. After two months of living in the new house I thought I was finally going to have a friend. Kate never changes. She acted the same way at camp.

In social studies, there was a huge message written on the chalkboard.

MAKE A DIFFERENCE.

"Class. Today I want to explain the annual seventh grade Make a Difference project," announced Miss Jenkins.

"You will be placed into groups according to a lottery. I entered your names into my computer and it chose the partners for the big project which will be due in the end of May. You will have to come up with your topics by the time you get back from Thanksgiving vacation. There will be other deadlines along the way."

I wondered who the computer chose to be my partner. I wanted to meet new kids at West Hills. It seemed they were already in groups and didn't want to include me. At least I had King and went to the stable to ride him after school.

"This project teaches you to care about your community and leads to a lifetime of service to others. It is so important, that you must get a passing grade in this project to pass seventh grade social studies. If you don't pass social studies, you won't proceed to eighth grade."

"Miss Jenkins, will we be winning prizes for the project?" It was Kate Baker talking out-of-turn. Was she always rude?

"Kate. Please raise your hand next time. Yes. The projects will be voted on by an independent panel of judges. There are many great prizes being donated by local stores and restaurants."

Miss Jenkins turned off the lights and turned on the projector. A video from the president of the United States talked about community service. There were stories about different people who had made a difference.

One middle school group started a bowling league at a senior citizens home. Another group cleaned up an area by a river and saved a duck that had a pop can plastic holder around his neck. The video showed kids washing the duck with blue dish soap.

The projector clicked off and the lights went back on. It didn't seem too hard. I had volunteered at a disabled children's horse riding therapy class back home. I was not sure what things were needed in my new community. Hopefully my partners and I would come up with good ideas.

"Now I will announce the groups you will work with."

Miss Jenkins read off all the partners. My name wasn't called yet.

"That does it for the groups of three. There are

only two more kids left and they will be the only group of two."

Oh, no. The only two left were myself and...

"Kate Baker and Jo Ann Elkavich. You are the last group. Jo Ann could you please come up here and pass out the sheet of guidelines for choosing a topic for the projects?" asked Miss Jenkins.

I handed out the papers. When I got to Kate, I said, "We need to get together to work on this."

"Have your people call my people," she said as she folded up the paper and put it in her notebook.

This was going to be a long school year.

Later that day, after dinner, the phone rang. Mrs. Smith had left her old-fashioned corded phones when she moved. Mom decided to keep them.

Maybe Kate had decided to get together to choose a project idea. I picked up the phone in the upstairs hall.

"Hello." My mom said. She had picked up the phone in the kitchen.

"Hi, beautiful," a man's voice said.

"Jo Ann, please hang up. Sir, you have the wrong number."

I hung up. I wondered if we had someone's old phone number.

When we moved to Northern Michigan from New York, my dad had just died. That was nine years ago when I was only three. Dad was in the Afghanistan war and was killed-in-action.

I tried to remember him. He was gone so much during my first three years, I had only a faint recollection of him. The only memories came from certain songs he sang and his voice saying, "Daddy's home," when he came in the door.

Mom joined the air force after dad died and moved us to Michigan so our Grandma could watch us. Granny was the elder on the reservation. Although she had many responsibilities, Aubra and I never felt neglected.

My school in the Upper Peninsula was small. There were only thirty kids in each grade. We had one classroom with the same kids every year. All the grades were in the same school.

We had our own horses and rode every day. We skied and skated in the winter and in the summer we swam, rode horses and danced in our tribe's Native American dance club. Mom would come home on leave as often as possible.

When I turned eight, I went to Camp Anishinabe all summer with Aubra. The first summer at camp I met Kate Baker. She made the two weeks at camp miserable when she was there She never let me play with her and her best friend, Stacey.

This past summer, when Stacey didn't show up, Kate and I became best friends. We had so much fun. She decided to stay two extra weeks. When Stacey showed up unexpectedly, Kate turned into a jealous freak and wouldn't talk to me.

Mom came to pick Aubra and I up at camp and

on the way home in the car she announced that she had a huge surprise for us.

"I have been released from my contract with the Air Force and they have helped me get an engineering position downstate. We will be moving into a house and we'll be a family again!"

"What! Mom you must be kidding. I am not moving away from my friends. And what will Granny do without us?" Aubra asked.

"Granny will be fine. She has a lot to do on the tribal council. We will go up north to visit her and she will come down to visit us."

"I think it's so cool. This is great, Mom. Where are we moving?" I asked.

"It's a beautiful, two-story, brick house on a corner lot," Mom's voice got very quiet, almost a whisper, "about six houses away from the Bakers."

"No way. I don't want to live near Kate. She was so mean this summer. Will I be going to the same school as her?"

"Yes, you'll go to West Hills Middle School. It's a great school with so many fun classes. Aubra will go to Lincoln High. Most importantly, we will be together as a family, again," Mom said.

I couldn't argue with that. I was happy we would be together. And having our own house was exciting.

"Will I have to share a room with the punk anymore?" asked Aubra.

"You girls will each have your own room to decorate any way you want."

"Finally I won't have to share a room with you, Jo Ann," Aubra said.

Hallelujah! I would finally have privacy.

Living near and going to school with Kate wasn't so bad since I got to have my own room and live with my mom.

Kate had no idea that we had moved into the old Smith house. It was hysterical when she walked by as we were unloading the moving van. Her jaw hit the floor. For the first time ever, Kate Baker was speechless. Since school started Kate had done everything possible to avoid me.

We would have to turn in our topic for our Make a Difference project the day after Thanksgiving vacation. Every time I tried to talk to her about it for the next couple of weeks, she avoided me. She was not going to make me fail Social Studies.

"We need to get the house clean and finish decorating the guest room before Grandma comes down for Thanksgiving," said Mom.

"Can I be in charge of decorating it, please, Mom?" I asked.

"Sure, Jo Ann. I'll have Aubra take you to the home store to pick out the bedding and some wall decorations. What color are you going to paint the room?"

"I get to paint it myself? That is so cool." When we moved in, Mom had professional painters come in.

"I can't decide on a color for the guest room. I will have to do it later," Mom said when she started her job. She had not had time to finish the decorating.

I was upstairs painting the guest room after school when the phone rang.

"Aubra, can you get that?" I yelled.

The phone rang again. I heard the water running. She must have been taking a shower. I put the roller down in the pan and answered the phone.

"Hello." No one responded but I thought I heard engines in the background. "Hello, is anyone there?" I asked. The phone went dead.

It must have been the wrong number. I went back to painting.

Later that week when the paint in the guest room was dry, I made the beds with the new sheets and comforters and then I hung the artwork.

"Hey, squirt. You did a good job painting. I didn't think it would look so good. I like the picture of the turtle. It reminds me of finding Kate on top of her backpack like an upside-down turtle," said Aubra.

"What? When did that happen?"

"Last month. I found her on the ground when I was driving to school. She couldn't get up. Her backpack was too heavy."

"All our bags are heavy." They were hard to carry every day. "Is that the day I saw you drop Kate off at school? Why were you so late that day?

Were you skipping school? Mom told you not to skip."

"You ask too many questions. Don't say anything to mom."

"I won't tell."

"Jo Ann, can you please set the table for dinner?" Mom was cooking the turkey and boiling the potatoes for Thanksgiving dinner. "The cloth is on the table. Could you please put out the good china and silver? I have it ready to go on the breakfront. Dinner will be ready soon."

I was setting out the plates. Grandma was at the kitchen table fussing over the flower arrangements. Since they got here yesterday, she and her sister, Aunt Anna, had been busy baking their famous pies. I was named after Aunt Anna and my grandpa, Joe.

"Mom why are there nine place settings? There are only five of us," I said

"The Bakers are joining us for dinner."

Kate, the traitor, hadn't talked to me or even looked at me since Halloween. Now I had to have her at my house for Thanksgiving dinner. That stunk.

The doorbell rang. Aubra opened the door and in walked the Baker Family. When everyone was hugging and saying hello, Kate didn't look at me.

"Welcome to the neighborhood. It's great to have old friends as neighbors. I am looking forward to our girls growing up together. We have so much to be thankful for this year," Kate's dad raised his glass and everyone but Kate clinked their glasses together.

After dinner my mom said, "Jo Ann. Why don't you take Kate upstairs and show her your room?"

Kate grunted as she followed me upstairs.

"This is my room. I decorated it myself. That's my dreamcatcher collection above my bed." I pointed to the circles of willow branches with red yarn and beads woven in a spider-web pattern. The feathers strung to the branches hung down on the wall. I loved the way they swayed with the breeze when the windows were open or when I opened and closed my door.

"What's a dreamcatcher?"

"The dreamcatcher is a symbol of unity among the Indian Nations. In our family we hang them above our beds to protect us from nightmares."

"How does that work?"

"It changes the person's dreams. Good dreams filter through the beads and webs of yarn and slide down the feathers to the sleeping person. The bad dreams stay in the net and in the morning they go out the window."

"Wow, that is so cool!"

"I made them myself. I can teach you. You can come over tomorrow since we have no school."

"Okay," said Kate.

When Kate arrived Friday we were still tidying up from the turkey dinner.

"Have you ever made a wish on a wishbone Kate?" asked my Aunt Anna as she pointed to the wishbone on the kitchen counter.

"No, I can't say that I ever have, Anna," said Kate.

"You and Jo Ann each hold one end of the wishbone and make a wish. Then pull until it breaks. The girl holding the biggest piece gets her wish," said Granny.

We each grabbed an end of the wishbone and pulled. It broke exactly in half.

"Does this mean we both get our wishes?" I asked.

"Yes, said Aunt Anna. Both of your wishes will come true if you don't tell each-other what you wished," said Granny.

I wasn't particularly superstitious, but I didn't tell Kate what I wished.

We went down in the basement to work on our dreamcatchers. I had set up the supplies before Kate arrived. The willow reeds were soaking in water and the dyed yarn was drying on the clothesline.

"What do we do first?" asked Kate.

"Take a reed and make it into a circle, then use the red yarn to tie the ends together. After that, weave the remaining length of yarn into a spider web pattern across the willow circle. Every so often, string one of these beads onto the yarn. Kind of like the necklace you made me at camp," I said.

"How big should I make this?" Kate asked.

"If you have a lot of bad dreams, you can make it big. Or you can make a couple of small ones. Whatever you like."

We worked on our dreamcatchers for a while. When it came time, we attached the feathers.

"I like this. It turned out beautiful. Thanks for teaching me. I can't wait to hang it over my bed," said Kate. "I guess I should go home now."

I walked Kate upstairs.

"I have to go to the stable to exercise and feed King and some of the other horses. You can come keep me company. Go home and change into your riding boots. Mom and I will pick you up in a few minutes," I told Kate.

Mom dropped us off at the Riding Club. I could tell Kate was angry about something. She always had a problem with me.

"First we have to muck out the stables. I have to take care of King and the next three horses. There is an extra bucket and shovel on the wall. If we get done fast we can go for a ride," I said.

Kate gave me a nasty look.

"You are so lucky. You have everything. You have your own horse."

"I'm not that lucky. I love riding King a few times a week and on Saturday, but the truth is, I don't like cleaning the stables. I have to do it so the price for boarding him can be cut down since my mom doesn't make enough money. You have a mom and a dad to pay the bills. You are the lucky one, Kate."

Kate left King's stall and took the shovel and bucket from the wall and began mucking out the other stalls and brushing Jersey and Nate, the other horses. I took care of King and Ella. We were done in no time.

"May I ride Jersey? She seems to like me," asked Kate.

"Sure. Saddle her up and I'll get King ready," I replied.

We rode out through the corral and onto the trail.

"We have passed this place many times, and I never knew there were trails behind here," said Kate.

After about thirty minutes we went back to the stable and watered and groomed King and Jersey. Then we saddled up Nate and Ella. We rode out to the trails again. Kate was silent the entire time.

"Are you still jealous, Kate? I love horses but they are a lot of work."

"I wish I had a horse. Do you think your aunt and uncle would let me have a horse next year?"

"Are you saying you will go to Camp Anishinabe next summer?"

"No. I'm never going back there. I hated it. You ruined camp for me. You stole my best friend. Now you're trying to steal Susan and Emily from me at Monday Night School. I hate you, you stink!"

Before I had a chance to answer her accusations, Kate dismounted from Nate's back and stalked off the trail. I grabbed his bridle and pulled him back to the stable. After taking the saddles off both horses, I quickly brushed them. Mom would be there to pick us up in a few minutes.

I went to the driveway where Mom was waiting in our van. Kate was sitting in the back seat. I opened the front door, sat down and put my seat belt on. No one said a word all the way home.

We dropped Kate off at her house. Once again, she wasn't talking to me. In two days school would start again and we still hadn't come up with a topic for our Make a Difference project.

Granny and Aunt Anna left Saturday morning to drive back up north. Mom and I spent most of the day on Saturday and Sunday raking leaves. Both days I went to the stable to take care of the horses.

Sunday night I got into bed early. I was super tired. It was going to be a busy week. I fell asleep right away.

In the middle of the night, I awoke suddenly. I looked at my clock. It was half past three. I thought I heard a voice coming from downstairs. Then it sounded like the front door shut. The beads on my dreamcatchers made a plinking noise as they bounced lightly against the wall.

I hopped out of bed to look out the window. Thick fog was sitting low to the ground. I thought I saw the figure of a man walking down the street.

My imagination was playing tricks on me. It

was probably the shadow of the large oak on our lawn and the sounds must have come from the blowing wind.

I got into bed, lay my head on the pillow and closed my eyes. I dreamt I was a baby. I was being thrown up in the air again and again. Each time I laughed and laughed. The webs in my dreamcatchers had caught the bad dreams and the good dreams floated down like feathers.

CHAPTER 4
THE DECEMBER DILEMMA

It was the first Monday of December. November ended with a bang. I hoisted my heavy backpack on my shoulder and made my way toward the bus stop over the hill and across the bridge. It was getting colder each morning, but I would never go to the Cabbage's bus stop. She would always be my enemy.

The day went by without any problems. Even Miss Tibble didn't pick on me. The teachers were tired from the long weekend. I dreaded going to seventh hour. It was the only class I had with The Cabbage. I sure didn't want to see her.

Miss Jenkins had the groups hand in their topics in Social Studies. "Kate and Jo Ann. You are the only students who didn't hand in your assignment. You will have an incomplete until I get your topic."

When the bell rang at the end of the day, I quickly left the classroom. I only had a minute to get to my locker and to the bus. When I walked past the social studies classroom I noticed The Cabbage was standing at Miss Jenkin's desk. She was probably blaming the incomplete on me. It wasn't my fault that she was a friend stealer. I wished she never moved here.

At Monday Night School, The Cabbage was sitting at the table with Susan, Emily and Elliot. I walked right by them and sat in an empty chair at another seventh grade table.

The kids gave me a surprised look. I acted like it was perfectly natural to sit with them. Three of them went to Mitzvah Club with me on Wednesdays.

Mitzvah Club started one year before our thirteenth birthdays. We studied the Hebrew parts we would be chanting and reciting during our Bar or Bat Mitzvah service.

Sarah was talking about the Hebrew teacher, Mr. Levine. "He gives us a ton of homework."

"Our bar and bat mitzvahs weren't until next school year, so I don't take him too seriously," said Lenny.

Sitting through dinner with the Mitzvah Club kids wasn't as much fun as sitting with Susan and Emily, but I could certainly do without the nerd, Elliot, and the stinky Cabbage.

Tuesday, after school, I could barely carry my backpack onto the bus, off the bus and all the way home. I got to gymnastics and had to sit out of most of the stunts. My back was killing me. The coach told me to rest and lay on a heating pad until Thursday's class.

Wednesday morning my back was still hurting. As I was packing my books up for the day, I decided to leave my science book at home. It was the heaviest book in my bag. We mostly used our lab workbooks, so I thought I was safe not bringing it.

"Students. Put everything away except your

textbook," said Miss Tibble. "We are having an open-book pop quiz."

I looked around. Everyone but Elliot Einstein was sitting at the lab tables with their textbooks open waiting for instructions. Elliot didn't bring his book. He knew everything about science without opening a book.

Miss Tibble was handing out the quiz sheets. She stopped at my desk.

"Miss Baker. Where is your textbook?" she asked.

"Uh, I think it is in my locker."

"Go upstairs to your locker and get it. Take the hall pass from my desk and get back here quickly."

Going to my locker wouldn't help. I left my science book at home. I needed to come up with a plan.

I went to the girl's lavatory on the second floor and hid in the stall. I held my feet up so no one would know I was in there. I heard the door open and peeked out through the crack of the stall door. Mallory and Kelsey were standing at the sinks looking in the mirrors at themselves and applying lipstick. I always tried to avoid them. They were so mean.

When the girls left the mirrors and went into the stalls, I snuck out quietly. Kelsey's science book was sitting on the shelf above the sink. She was in science during a different hour. I grabbed her book and went out the door as fast as possible. I ran down the stairs, down the hall and into the science room.

My heart was pounding in my chest. I didn't really steal her book. I borrowed it. I opened the classroom door, threw the hall pass on the teacher's desk and sat at my lab table.

I turned to the correct chapter in Kelsey's book and started taking the quiz. I finished the quiz and left it and the hall pass on Miss Tibble's desk on my way to lunch.

I put Kelsey's book in my locker and grabbed my lunch bag. On the way to my regular lunch table, I walked past Mallory's table. I couldn't help overhearing her conversation.

"I don't know who stole your book, Kelsey, but we will find out. When we do, that person will be in big trouble," said Mallory.

I couldn't eat my lunch. My stomach was hurting. Mallory was so mean. If she found out I took Kelsey's book, she would kill me. Then she would make fun of me forever.

I asked the lunch lady for a pass to leave the lunchroom to go to the lavatory. I knew what the rule was during lunch; you had to use the bathroom on the first floor. I couldn't go on the first floor. I had to go to my locker on the second floor.

I snuck up the back stairs. I hid behind the big pillar at the top of the steps. I peeked around the corner. No one was in the hall-way. The classroom doors were all closed. I tip-toed to my locker.

I quietly turned the tumbler on my

combination lock. Thirteen to the right, eight to the left and twenty-six to the right. When the lock disengaged, I lifted the hinge as quietly as possible.

I took Kelsey's book out of my locker, carefully and silently lifted the hinge, closed the locker door and turned the tumbler. I couldn't take a chance that it would make noise. As I was walking away from my locker, an eighth grader from my neighborhood named William came out from the classroom across the hall. He had a pass in his hand. I put my head down and turned away so he wouldn't recognize me.

"Hi, Kate," he said.

I didn't answer. So much for not being noticed.

I walked quickly down the hall and into the lavatory. I placed Kelsey's book on the shelf above the sink, just where it had been when I borrowed it. The bell rang signaling the end of seventh grade lunch hour. I went into the stall. I had to pee so bad.

When I left the stall to wash my hands, Mallory and Kelsey walked through the door.

"Look at that! Someone left their science book in the bathroom," I said as I dried my hands on a paper towel.

I opened the cover of the textbook. "Oh, look, Kelsey. It has your name in it," I said.

"Kate Baker, did you have something to do with this? If I find out you stole Kelsey's book I will get even with you," said Mallory.

"Why doesn't Kelsey speak for herself?"

I left the lavatory quickly and went to my locker. It was a narrow escape.

The last three hours of school went off without a hitch. In social studies, Miss Jenkins didn't mention the Make a Difference project. We finished up with the Pilgrims and Native Americans right before Thanksgiving and we were starting the 1700's and the birth of our nation.

If I could get out of trouble with Miss Tibble so easily, I could come up with a way to get out of trouble with Miss Jenkins. I would have to go see her after school.

I would try to get out of The Cabbage's group and into a group that already had a topic. The Cabbage could do the Make a Difference project by herself.

When I got home from school, the house was quiet. I ate my snack and was starting my homework when the doorbell rang.

"Who is it?" I asked through the wooden door.

"I am taking a survey for the United States Census. Can you answer a few questions about your neighbors?" The man asked from the other side of the closed door.

He was tall and looked very clean. He had a badge hanging from his neck. Although I couldn't read the name through the glass of the storm door, the picture on the badge matched his face.

I wasn't supposed to open the door to strangers, but he sounded and looked official.

"Do you know anything about the new people

that just moved in on the corner? The Elkavich family? From my records there is a mother with two daughters living there. Is there a man living with them?" he asked.

"No. Just the mother and daughters. No man lives there," I answered.

"So this Mrs. Elkavich isn't involved with any men at this time? You see we need a count of all the people living in each house. It is important for tax purposes," he said.

"No men live there."

Just then, mom drove up the driveway and into the garage. By the time she and Timmy came in the house, the man from the Census Bureau had walked down the sidewalk and disappeared around the corner.

Mom came in through the laundry room.

"Who was that at the door? What did he want? I told you not to answer the door when Dad or I aren't home."

"It was the United States Census worker. He had a badge. He wanted to know how many people live at the Elkavich house."

"I guess that sounds harmless. Please don't answer the door anymore if Dad or I aren't home."

"Okay, Mom. I won't answer it again." I figured this was a good time to ask her, "I am going to have to stay after school tomorrow. I have to talk to Miss Jenkins about my project. Will you pick me up after school tomorrow and take me to gymnastics?"

"Sure Kate. I'll bring you a healthy snack to eat on the way." My mom always could be depended on to keep me healthy.

On Thursday I stayed behind after the bell. I was standing by Miss Jenkin's desk. The Cabbage gave me the stink-eye as she was leaving.

"Kate do you have something to talk to me about?" she asked.

"Yes. I would like to be put in a different group for the Make a Difference project. Jo Ann Elkavich is not a good worker. She hasn't cooperated with me to choose a topic."

"That's interesting, Kate. Jo Ann met with me after school yesterday. She told me you weren't cooperating with her. I told her you two have to work out your differences.

These projects aren't done only to come up with ideas to help others. They are created to teach students to work in teams. You and Jo Ann will have to find a way to work together or you will not pass this class. If you don't have anything else to say to me, I have to get to the curriculum meeting," said Miss Jenkins.

"No. I have nothing else to say." I left the Social Studies room and went out to the parent's pick-up driveway.

"I don't feel well. Can we go home? My back is hurting. I can't go to gymnastics today."

"Okay, Kate. If your back doesn't feel better soon, we will have to go to the doctor," Mom said.

Friday morning there was a note in my locker. The teachers have the combination and can open your locker any time they want. It was a good thing I got rid of Kelsey's science book. I opened the note.

'Come to my office at 9:45 am today. Mrs. Saslove has been notified to let you leave art early. Be sure to take a hall pass.'

When I walked in the Counseling Center the secretary wasn't at her desk. I wrote my name on the first blank line on the sign-in sheet and sat in a chair against the wall. Did someone know I borrowed the science book from Kelsey? I was trying to figure out why she summoned me into her office when Mrs. Spyrka opened her door.

"Miss Baker, please come in. Have a seat," she said pointing at a sofa across from her desk. I sat on one end of the sofa. She sat on the other end.

"Kate, when new students come to our school, we like to make them feel at home. It is difficult for people in middle school to make new friends."

Oh no she didn't!

Mrs. Spyrka kept talking, "a new girl named Jo Ann Elkavich has been having a hard time..."

That two-faced Cabbage must have told on me.

"...making friends. I have noticed she is eating lunch by herself and hasn't been participating in any after-school activities."

So she didn't tell on me.

"I thought since you went to camp with her..."

How would the school counselor know I went

to camp with Jo Ann?

"...you could be nice to her and be her friend."

Mrs. Spyrka was ready to say more, so I interrupted her.

"I am not going to be Jo Ann's friend. She is not nice to me. She's stealing my friends at my temple just like she stole my best friend at camp. She's fooling you into thinking I am the problem. She has a horse!" I stormed out of Mrs. Spyrka's office without a hall pass.

Class was changing for third hour. I went to my locker and grabbed my apron for my skills for living class. I walked into the dietetics room. It was a huge space with eight fully functioning kitchens. Each kitchen had a table and chairs. There were four students assigned to each kitchen.

Mr. Titus was our cooking teacher. He was the head chef at a fancy restaurant at night. Everything we had cooked so far was delicious.

"Class. Today we will be starting our unit on soups. The first recipe we will be making can be served hot or cold. It has many healthy ingredients and is easy to make. The vegetables you will need are next to your sinks. Let's get busy with the Cabbage Soup," Mr. Titus said.

I couldn't get away from The Cabbage no matter how hard I tried.

I was happy it was Friday and the weekend would be starting soon. In social studies The Cabbage was staring at me. I looked away and totally ignored her. The final bell rang. I couldn't get out of school fast enough.

I went to my locker and grabbed my backpack. As I was loading it with all my books, I noticed I had forgotten my social studies book on my desk. I closed my locker and I went back in the classroom. No one was there. I walked over to my desk, picked up my book and put it in my backpack.

I raced out to the driveway where our busses lined up. Bus number 24 had just pulled away. Bus number 19 was just starting to pull away when the driver recognized me from the sixth grade. She stopped the bus and opened the door.

"C'mon Kate. You can ride home with us today."

I put my foot on the first step and hoisted myself and my heavy backpack up the other two steps. I stopped in the aisle to survey the empty seats.

"C'mon Kate. Sit down so we can get on the road," said the driver.

The one and only empty seat was next to The Cabbage. I rushed down the aisle as the bus started to move.

"Ouch," I screamed as I felt a sharp pain in my left thigh.

I reached down and put my hand on my jeans. There wasn't any blood, but there was a hole clean through the denim.

"That kid just stabbed Kate with a compass. I saw him do it," yelled The Cabbage. She was standing in the aisle pointing at Ron Bennington, an eighth-grader with a shaky reputation.

The bus driver pulled the bus over to the curb when he heard me scream. He walked down the aisle and put his hand on Ron's shoulder.

"Son, you are in a heap of trouble," he said as he escorted Ron off the bus.

Even though I knew the bus driver was outside, the bus seemed to be moving and spinning. The next thing I knew, I was lying on a gurney in the hospital emergency room. The Cabbage was standing over me on my left. My mom was standing on my right.

"You passed out from shock," said Mom. You'll be okay. The nurse will be in soon to give you a tetanus shot.

The only thing I hated more than spiders were needles.

"Why do I have to have a shot?"

The nurse came in through the curtain. "Young lady, you have a puncture wound. It didn't bleed. That's the most dangerous wound you can have. You will have to stay here until the intravenous antibiotic runs out."

I raised my right arm. There was a needle in my hand attached to long tube running up to a bag on a pole. I felt the room spinning.

"You came here in an ambulance. I got to ride with you," said The Cabbage.

"Ron Bennington said it was an accident. He was putting his compass in his backpack when you walked into the point on the way down the aisle of the bus. The police talked to him and said it seemed like he was telling the truth," Mom explained.

"Mrs. Baker, I don't think it was an accident. That kid is lying," said The Cabbage.

"He has been in trouble so many times, but he never has done anything wrong to me before," I said.

"If you say so, Kate. I'll be watching him from now on," said The Cabbage.

"I want to get out of here and go home before the nurse comes back with the shot."

"You're not going anywhere, Honey," said the nurse. She pinched my upper arm and plunged the ten-inch long, sharp steel needle into my flesh.

I survived the ordeal of being stabbed by a compass and a tetanus shot. On the way home from the hospital we dropped The Cabbage off at her house.

"Good night, Pickle. I hope you feel better soon." She hadn't called me Pickle since we were best friends at camp.

"Good night Cabbage."

Saturday morning my arm was sore from the tetanus shot and my leg was sore from being stabbed. It hurt to walk, but my parents made me go to services at the temple with them. When we got home the phone was ringing. My brother ran to answer it.

"Hello, Baker residence, Timmy speaking."

Timmy thought he was so cool.

"Kate it's Jo Ann for you."

"Hi, Jo Ann."

"How is your leg?"

"Okay. It hurts a bit."

"I went to the stables this morning to exercise King. Would you like to go to the mall? I have to buy a few Chanukah gifts. My mom said she'll drive there if your parents pick up."

"Chanukah gifts! For who?"

"I thought told you my dad was Jewish. We are going to see my dad's mom in New York for a few days before the holiday break. Then we're going to the Upper Peninsula to see Granny for Christmas."

She was lucky to miss a few days of school. We weren't going anywhere for break. It was going to be boring.

"I didn't know you were half and half. My mom was Catholic. She converted when she and Dad got married. Now both my parents are Jewish. My relatives in Canada don't even know what Chanukah is!"

"Wow, Pickle. We have a lot in common."

"Yes, Cabbage. Let's go to the mall."

My mom made a big deal about me having a sore leg and walking too much at the mall. Dad told her to let me go.

While Dad was in a good mood I asked him,

"Can I have some money to go Chanukah shopping?" I didn't want to use up all of my babysitting money.

"Sure, Kate. Here are two twenties. Is that enough?"

I took the money.

"Thanks, Daddy. I love you."

"I love you, too, Pumpkin."

Things never changed. Dad always called me Pumpkin.

We went to every store at the mall. In between stores, we went to the food court. I ordered my favorite, a Greek salad with grilled chicken.

I bought a pair of earrings for Mom, a tie for Dad and a stocking cap with a lion on it for Timmy. I didn't have to spend any of my babysitting money. My Chanukah shopping was done.

The Cabbage said, "I got all of my shopping done. I even bought a Christmas brooch for Granny and a pair of fluffy socks for Aunt Anna."

"It's getting late. I still have some homework to finish before I babysit for the Cohens tonight," I said.

"I love little kids. Can I come babysitting with you?"

"I'll call and ask."

Mrs. Cohen said it was fine if my friend came with me. The Cabbage came over a few minutes before Mr. Cohen drove up to take us to his house.

The Cabbage brought a bag full of puzzles. We played some board games while the twins were busy fitting the puzzle pieces together.

Mrs. Cohen called to say good night to the

boys. Later when the kids were in bed, The Cabbage and I watched a movie on television.

During the movie, The Cabbage told me about the wrong numbers and hang ups she was getting at her house.

"I've also heard weird sounds at night. I think it may be the wind. I am not sure," she said worriedly.

"It sounds like nothing." I thought about mentioning the Census taker. Then the movie got to a good part and we dropped the subject.

It was fun to have company while babysitting. It was usually so boring after the kids went to bed. I didn't fall asleep on the couch like I did when I was alone.

"Bryan and Ryan loved having two babysitters tonight," said Mrs. Cohen when she and her husband came back from their 'date.' "May I have your phone number, Jo Ann, in case Kate can't sit one night?"

"Sure Mrs. Cohen. Here it is," The Cabbage said as she wrote her number in the Cohen's address book.

She had stooped low in the past. Dancing with Nick Caputo, stealing The Pilgrim and the girls at Monday Night School. Now this was going too far.

Mr. Cohen dropped her off first.

"Good night, Kate" said The Traitor.

I looked straight out the front windshield of the car. No one tried to steal my babysitting job and stayed my friend.

"Kate. It is the day before holiday break and you still haven't handed in your topic for the Make a Difference project."

"Miss Jenkins. You see, it isn't my fault. Jo Ann hasn't been cooperative. She isn't even here today. She left school three days ago. Maybe she will get her act together when school starts in January." I turned away and sat at my desk.

The day after the holiday break started, my parents loaded up the car to go to Florida to see Bubby and Zayde, Dad's parents.

"This was a last minute decision," Dad said after we dropped Seska and the iguanas off at the kennel. Mom had Allie in her pocket. It was hard to find anyone to watch an alligator. "Mom and I thought you and Timmy could use some fun in the sun."

Mom and Dad took turns driving all day until we reached the half-way point in Tennessee. We stayed in a motel over night. Allie slept in the bathroom sink.

We got up early the next morning and drove all day. We stopped occasionally at rest areas to stretch our legs and use the restrooms. Mom came well equipped with sandwiches and other healthy foods in a cooler.

"Mom do we have any junk food in the cooler? I really could go for some candy or cookies," I commented while mom was taking her turn driving.

"Kate, I have carrot sticks and low-fat cheese cubes," said Mom.

"Can't we eat something different on a trip?" asked Timmy. It is Hanukkah.

"What is this? You want some special Chanukah treats?" asked Dad. "I just happen to have chocolate coins and dreidel cookies for each of you," he said as he handed each of us a bag. Dad has always had the biggest sweet tooth in our family.

"Woo hoo!" exclaimed Timmy as he tore open the mesh bag of gold-foil covered chocolate coins.

I saw mom looking at me in the rear view mirror. She smiled and I smiled back.

We reached Bubby and Zayde's house on Sanibel Island late at night. Dad had a key so we snuck in quietly and went to the rooms we always slept in when we visited.

The next morning the sun flooded through the window. What a beautiful day! I felt like a new girl.

My cousins were already there. They came from every corner of the country to visit the "Baker's Dozen Resort" as Bubby called her house on the island. Dad, his two sisters and one brother had twelve kids among them.

There was a huge breakfast buffet set up on the long kitchen island. My cousins and their parents were waking up in intervals. As they arrived in the kitchen, they took plates of food to tables inside the house and outside to the lanai, the screened-in porch next to the pool.

Our cousins, Timmy, and I celebrated the nights of Chanukah that were left. We played on the beach or by the pool during the day. At night we played board games and watched old movies. The whole family, all twenty-two of us hung out. It was loud with everyone talking at the same time.

I was alone in the bedroom watching a show on television when a Public Service Announcement came on. "The United States Bureau of Census wants to be sure every person is counted. We will notify you by mail if your census form is incomplete. We will not come to your door to complete the census. Remember, we will only ask about you, we will never ask about your neighbors. If this should happen, immediately report to the number on the screen. Call 1-800-You-Count."

I had a strange feeling that the census worker who came to my house was an imposter. Why would someone be asking about the Elkavich family? I didn't want to talk to The Cabbage about it, but I might have to tell Aubra.

While we were in Florida, Allie died.

"It doesn't make any sense that an alligator from Florida would live two years in Michigan, and die in her homeland," I said through sniffles. I couldn't help crying.

"Alligators aren't made for pets," said Zayde.

My Grandpa never minced words. He just told it as it was. Although I was sad, he made sense. Allie was never cuddly like a dog or cat. She never acted happy to see us or even acknowledged our presence. All she did was stand still in one place on the raised plastic island in the turtle bowl, or float on the water in the river surrounding the plastic island.

I didn't get any alone-time with Bubby and Zayde while we were on our vacation. There were too many people to pay attention to. I had fun at first, but after a few days it got a bit annoying and claustrophobic.

Timmy was having a blast with all the cousins. He didn't want to leave when it came time. I was happy to pack into our car and head home. I couldn't wait to start the New Year.

CHAPTER 5
TO SKI OR NOT TO SKI

There was a huge snow storm the last day of holiday break. I thought we would have a snow day, but the plows came out in force and school started on time.

I wore my boots every day and had to carry an extra bag with my platform shoes to wear during school. Even though I had so much to carry, I trudged through the snow to the other bus stop to avoid going to the Elkavich house. Seeing The Cabbage as little as possible was my ultimate New Year's resolution.

When we got home from Florida, my schedule for second semester was in the mailbox. First semester still had two weeks left. At the end of the first semester, we would have midterm exams in all the classes.West Hills Middle School was trying to kill me.

Then report cards would come out. We had not turned in our Make a Difference topic. The Cabbage and I were going to get an incomplete in social studies.

Some of the groups had already begun their projects. Elena, Risa and Alan were making weekly visits to the zoo to feed the penguins. Vinnie, Mike and Jen were going to the library every Saturday to read to little kids.

At the temple on Wednesday, the Cantor told me I should start planning my Mitzvah Project. He told me many West Hills students used their Make a Difference projects as their Mitzvah Projects. I didn't tell him it was hard to come up with a topic when you didn't talk to your project partner.

Two weeks off without carrying the heavy backpack cured me. My back wasn't hurting when school started. After a week and a half of gymnastics and carrying my backpack, my back started to hurt again.

Ski Club was starting and I wanted to join. I kept going to gymnastics. I didn't tell my mom my back hurt.

Ski Club would meet on six Wednesdays starting in the middle of January and go until the end of February. Since I had Mitzvah Club on Wednesdays after school, I had to convince my parents how important Ski Club was to my social life.

"Dad, I want to join the ski club. Can I miss Mitzvah Club for six weeks? I'm doing great on my torah portion and everyone is joining Ski Club."

"Kathryn, I don't have time to discuss this now. I have to go into the social hall and address the Monday Nighters. We will have to talk later. And besides, you don't know how to ski."

"I'll learn fast."

"I'll talk to your mom. She has to make the final decision since she will be picking you up," Dad said.

The next day, I went to the office with a check in my hand for the Ski Club. Mom and Dad agreed that I needed to do more school activities. They said they'd pay for the Ski Club, but I had to go to the ski shop and buy some used skis with my babysitting money.

"As far as Mitzvah Club goes, you will have to practice at home and meet with the Cantor during Monday Night School to go over what you miss each week," Dad explained.

"Dad, you're the best. I can't wait to go skiing," I said as I gave him a peck on the cheek.

The Snow Peak Ski Shop was on the corner of the highway in the shopping center. I trudged through the snow in the Matthews' yard to avoid passing by The Cabbage's house.

The used skis were in the back of the store. I found some boots in my size. Luckily there were skis to go with them.

"I don't think the person who owned these skis used them very much. They look like brand new," said the sales lady.

"Are there any ski poles to go with these?"

"As a matter of fact, there are some that came with those skis. Yes, here they are," she said as she pulled them out of the stand behind the register.

"So how much does all of this come to?" I showed her my coupon. I hoped I would have enough to cover the cost.

"With your coupon and the used ski discount it comes to sixty-seven dollars even."

"Here you are." I gave her three twenties and a ten. Babysitting was paying off.

"And here is your change. Do you need any help with those?"

"No, thanks, I can manage."

I picked up my skis, poles and boots. When I turned around to go toward the door, I knocked over a big display of hats and gloves. "Sorry," I said.

Carrying skis was awkward. I was going to have to be more careful. I had to look like I skied before. I didn't want anyone to think I was a beginner.

It seemed a lot farther going home than it did on the way up to the store. When I got home, I put my ski stuff in the mudroom and got busy doing my homework. I was so excited about ski club, I couldn't concentrate.

I went online. There was a lot more to skiing than I thought. Tow ropes and chair-lifts and bunny hills for beginners.

I wouldn't need to go on the bunny hill. I was going right to the advanced hill. I read up about skiing until I was sure I knew all there was to know. No problem, I thought. I will look like a pro.

The days dragged by until the first Wednesday of Ski Club. My mom drove me to school that morning, since it was pretty hard to take all my ski equipment on the bus.

"You're lucky it's snowing today. Make sure you start out on the bunny hill," said mom.

"Mom, it's not that hard to ski. I will be fine. I'll see you later."

We stored our ski equipment in the back of the

janitor's closet until the bus picked us up to take us to the ski resort. I couldn't concentrate in my classes. All I could think about was how much fun I would have skiing after school.

I looked like an official skier with my ski-lift ticket attached to my zipper. I lined up with the others waiting for the Ski Express bus. There were mostly eighth graders and a few seventh and sixth graders in the club

I couldn't believe my eyes. The Cabbage was right there in line! She ruined everything. It was bad enough that she tried to steal my babysitting job, I had to do the Make a Difference project with her, and she comes to Monday Night School. Now I had to put up with her at ski club. It was going to be agony.

"Hi, Kate. Your mom will be driving us home today, My mom will be picking us up next week," said The Cabbage.

"I wasn't apprised of that. There must be some mistake," I said.

Well, that's just great. Why did my mom have to complicate everything? She always had to arrange car-pools. She knew I hated The Cabbage.

"I'll see you later," I told The Cabbage as I went to sit in the back of the bus.

The teacher who was in charge was telling us the rules as we drove to the ski resort. Always more rules. I was half listening while I looked out the window. I thought I heard him say, "and we will meet at the bus at promptly seven o'clock sharp."

We left our backpacks on the bus. Mom told me to take a snack, and I did, but I forgot it in my locker. I was so hungry. I headed to the snack shop.

While in the line to buy something to eat, I looked out the window. I saw The Cabbage holding onto the tow rope headed toward the advanced hill. There was no way I was going to let her think she was a better skier than me. I left the snack bar line and went outside.

I hooked my skis to my boots. I stood up and started walking toward the tow rope, and my skis stayed on the ground.

"Can you please help me?" I asked the ski resort worker who was walking toward me.

"Sure. You have to attach this part first and then buckle this."

"Thanks," I said.

"If you are a beginner, you should go to the bunny hill first. They have instructors to help you," he said.

"Oh, I am not a beginner. I ski all the time. These are new skis, my old ones were all worn out," I fibbed as I headed toward the tow rope for the advanced hill.

I held onto the rope. It started pulling me up the hill. My skis stayed stuck in the snow and my body kept going uphill. Soon I was horizontal.

The kid behind me said, "stand up straight and straighten your skis."

I did what he suggested and it wasn't so hard after all. I used my ski poles to propel myself toward the chair lifts. It was quite a steep hill. I watched a few people get off and on the chair lifts. They had to ski down the hill as soon as they got off. It looked easy enough. If they could do it, I could do it.

The line in front of me was getting shorter as two by two, people were getting on the chair lifts. You had to stand with your back to the chair and grab onto the side as the chair scooped you up.

I shuffled over when it was my turn. I was so fixated on how I was going to get on the chair, I didn't notice that The Cabbage was right beside me.

"C'mon Kate, get going, it's our turn," she said as she pushed me toward the empty wooden bench coming at us at quite a fast speed.

"I'm ready," I said, just as the chair hit me from behind.

"Grab on right now," said The Cabbage. "You've never skied before, have you, Kate?"

"Of course I have skied. I ski all the time."

I heard The Cabbage sigh. I was just about to say something to her when I looked down. I couldn't believe I was sitting on the chairlift with my legs dangling in mid-air. We were up pretty high going toward the top of a very tall hill, covered in snow.

When we got to the top of the hill, the chair lift paused and a ski resort worker held onto it while

The Cabbage got off. I was petrified, but I wouldn't give her the satisfaction of seeing that I didn't know what I was doing, and that I had never skied before in my life.

"I forgot something, I can't get off here," I said to the resort worker.

There wasn't much time to argue. The chairs kept moving. I stayed in my seat and watched The Cabbage pull her ski goggles down on her face and away she went down the hill. She didn't act like she cared that I wasn't getting off the chair lift!

By the time the chair lift reached the bottom of the hill, I was angry. I couldn't believe I let The Cabbage see me scared. When the ride ended, I asked the ski worker if I could stay on. A boy named James, who I knew from West Hills, got on the chair lift with me. We rode to the top of the hill in silence.

"Well, are you getting off this time?" the worker on top of the hill asked as he held onto the chair while James got off.

"Nope, I think I will ride down again, I think I am going to buy a snack," I answered.

He didn't say anything as my chair and I rode down the hill again.

I kept staying on the chair-lift, half because I was trying to get enough nerve to ski down the big hill at the top and half because I didn't have the nerve to ski down the little hill at the bottom.

My legs were numb, frozen and sore from hanging in mid-air in the cold. Finally, after about ten trips around and around, I jumped off at the bottom. I slipped and slid part-way down the hill until I was able to stop. There was no way I was going to ski the rest of the way down the slippery slope, so I walked side-ways down the hill using my ski poles to balance until I reached the snack shop.

It was dark out. I sat on the bench and unlatched my skis from my boots. I left my skis in the rack and I went inside. I was starving.

I got in line and bought some hot chocolate and a hot dog. I sat down at a table to eat. I looked around to see if there were any familiar kids. I glanced at the clock. It was seven-twenty three. Oh, no. The bus was supposed to leave at seven o'clock sharp!

I left everything on the table and ran outside to the driveway. There were no buses from our school district waiting in the line.

I couldn't believe it. They left without me! That witch, The Cabbage, didn't come looking for me. She just went home with everyone else and abandoned me! To make matters worse, my backpack was on the bus!

I walked through the snack shop and out the back door. I was crying. I plopped down on the bench next to the rack where my skis were. If I called my parents, they would come to pick me up, but I wouldn't be able to stand their lecturing. And Timmy would tease me forever.

"Here you are. We've been looking for you. The

whole ski club is on the bus waiting for you." The Cabbage was standing behind me and looking down on me with her, 'I knew you didn't know how to ski,' smirk on her face.

I stood up and wiped the tears off my face before she had a chance to see I had been crying.

"Well, are you going to stand there all day or are you going to get on the bus so we can leave?" The Cabbage asked as she walked toward the door.

All the snow had melted. The next two Wednesdays Ski Club was cancelled due to unseasonably warm temperatures. I went to Mitzvah Club instead.

I managed to avoid The Cabbage during Social Studies. There was no mention of the Make a Difference project as we were spending class time reviewing for mid-term exams.

My back was killing me. On Tuesdays and Thursdays I couldn't go to gymnastics. Mom took me to the doctor.

"Kate, you have a bulging disc in your back," said the doctor as he looked at my x-ray. "You are going to have to stop gymnastics for a while. Skiing is out-of-the question."

"What will I do about gym class in school?"

"I'll write you a note to excuse you from gym. You won't be able to carry a heavy backpack to school. You'll need to put your books in a rolling suitcase. Pick up a prescription for physical therapy at the front desk. You will have to go twice a week."

The next day Mom drove me to school. It had snowed and there was no rolling a suitcase on the ice and snow. I would never have made it over the big hill on the way to bus number 24.

"Kate, I'll pick you up after school to go to physical therapy," Mom said as she dropped me off at the parents door. "Tomorrow you will have to take the bus. I can't drive you every day, you know."

There was no way I wanted to go to the bus stop at The Cabbage's house. I would have to ignore her all the way to school and back.

The rolling suitcase wouldn't fit in my locker. I was already late to class. The bell rang as I entered the principal's office.

"You can put your books inside your locker and leave the empty suitcase in front of your locker," said the secretary as she handed me a hall pass.

"I wouldn't have a back problem if this school didn't give us so many textbooks."

The secretary looked at me as if she had no clue.

I dragged my suitcase up the stairs, went to my locker, and then to Mr. Kulis's first-hour algebra class.

"Kids, I'm passing out your second semester schedules. This will give you a chance to see what classes you will attend next term. If there are any changes necessary, they must be requested in writing by your parents before the mid-term exams next Thursday," Mr. Kulis said.

During lunch, The Cabbage came up to me with her new schedule. "Kate, do you have second hour choir next semester? What is Mr. Balbes like?"

She was in two classes with me. Not only that, because of my sore back, I was going to have to go to her bus stop every day, and to Monday Night School every week.

My parents would have to write a note to get me changed out of choir. It was a shame since I loved singing and Mr. Balbes was a great teacher. We never had homework, and he let us sing all the latest hit songs.

"You know, Jo Ann, Mr. Balbes is the worst teacher. He is so mean. You won't like him. He never gives anyone higher than a 'C' no matter how hard you work," I went on, "and he gives hours and hours of homework every day. You have to do a ten page report on a different composer every weekend." The Cabbage could change classes instead of me. I ignored The Cabbage and went on eating my lunch. She walked away.

I waited on the corner in front of the Elkavich house every morning before school. It was cold, snowy and windy, but I didn't want to go into The Cabbage's house with the other kids.

By the time the bus came, the wheels of my suitcase were frozen solid. I had to carry the heavy load up the stairs of the bus. It was much better than my backpack, though.

I studied more than ever for mid-terms. I was

well prepared in each class. The exams were easier than I thought.

We used to bring paper report cards home. Some kids would throw them away or change the grades. Now the grades were sent to the parents on-line.

"Have you received my report card yet, Dad?" I asked on Friday after mid-terms.

"Yes, I did, Kate. You did well in all your classes. What is with the 'Incomplete' in Social Studies?"

"That stupid Jo Ann won't work with me on our Make a Difference project. She is always cancelling our meetings. I am sick of her."

"Kate. When you do a group project you have to cooperate. Now that you are going to less after-school activities and you're going to the same bus stop, you can ask Jo Ann to meet with you before or after school."

How did my dad know I wasn't going to The Cabbage's bus stop the first few months of school? I thought they never noticed me cutting through the Matthew's yard. The Cabbage or her sister, Aubra, must have told him about the upside-down turtle incident. I knew they were traitors.

"Okay, dad. I will try to get her to cooperate," I said.

That night there was a huge snowstorm. We couldn't shovel enough snow to get out of our driveway Saturday morning. The temple cancelled services. I had no homework since second semester hadn't started yet.

We couldn't go to the mall or anywhere all day. I rested and watched a lot of television. Mrs. Cohen called to cancel babysitting. It felt good to have a break.

By Sunday the road crews cleaned up the snow and things were back to normal. Dad went to Sunday school with Timmy. Mom and I spent the day baking special pastries for the upcoming Purim Carnival.

We experimented with new flavors like blackberry and triple chocolate. We shared a couple while they were still warm.

"Mom, these are the best hamentashen I ever ate," I said.

"That's because you are a good Baker!" Mom said laughing at her own joke. She hugged me and gave me a big kiss on the forehead.

"How is your back feeling?" asked Mom.

"I think physical therapy and not carrying the heavy backpack have helped. It feels a lot better."

"I am so proud of you, Kate. You have done well in school this year. I wish you and Jo Ann would get along. She lives so close, you should be best friends again."

"I don't need her for a friend."

I went upstairs to my room. I heard my mom sigh as she put the cooled off cookies in the freezer for the Purim Carnival.

Monday morning I went to the bus stop at The Cabbage's house. An icy January wind was blowing. My face was frozen by the time I got to the door. I wheeled my suitcase full of books onto her front porch. There were six kids waiting in her foyer.

"C'mon in, Kate. We have hot cocoa. It has cinnamon in it," The Cabbage said.

"Cinnamon. In hot cocoa?" I carefully sipped the hot drink. It was delicious.

When the bus came, I sat by myself. The Cabbage and the others sat together. She had made friends with the kids in our neighborhood.

CHAPTER 6
ON YOUR MARK, GET SET, SADIES!

The new semester was going well. I managed to avoid The Cabbage as much as possible. During choir, just to ruin my plan, Mr. Balbes paired The Cabbage and I up to sing a duet in the Spring Musical.

"You girls will have to practice outside of school. We want the numbers to be polished. All the seventh-grade families will be invited."

I wanted to change partners, and I think The Cabbage read my mind.

"Mr. Balbes, I don't think I can do this song," said The Cabbage.

"Jo Ann. You and Kate sound great. For the sake of the entire choir you have to stay in the groups I put you in."

"Mr. Balbes believes in us, Kate. Let's get together after school one day this week to practice," The Cabbage said.

"Maybe we should think of a project for Make a Difference, too," I said.

I went home with her after school the next day. I hadn't been further than her foyer since December. We grabbed a snack and went into her family room.

"We sound great," Jo Ann said after we practiced the song a couple times. "My mom had a good idea. If your back is getting better, would you like to take turns going to the stable to take care of

King and ride him a couple times a week?"

I was about to answer her when the phone rang and she picked it up.

"Hello, this is Jo Ann. Yes, Mrs. Cohen, I can sit for you next week," she said.

That was all I needed to hear. I grabbed my suitcase and coat and wheeled out the front door and down the street to my house. The Cabbage was infiltrating every part of my existence. Now she was stealing my babysitting job.

We still hadn't picked a project for the Social Studies class. I didn't care anymore. I may have to go on the same bus and to Monday Night School and sing a song in the Spring Musical with her, but I was not going to spend one more minute doing a project with the stinky Cabbage.

When I got home, the phone was ringing. I heard my mom answer it.

"Kate it's for you."

"If it's Jo Ann, tell her to jump off a cliff," I said.

"Hello," I said when I picked up the extension in the hallway upstairs.

"Kate, this is Jessica Cohen. I just spoke to Jo Ann. I am having a friend come from out of town next Saturday night. She's bringing her two children. I'd like both of you to sit since four kids are a bit much for one sitter."

I felt terrible. I shouldn't have left in a huff. The Cabbage didn't steal my job, after all.

"Mr. Cohen will pick both of you girls up at

your houses and bring you here at the usual six-ish."

"I'm sorry, Mrs. Cohen. I am busy that night."

The next day when I saw The Cabbage she said, "Since you are busy Aubra will go with me next Saturday to sit for the Cohens. I told Mrs. Cohen I can't sit anymore after that. I didn't want to intrude on your job."

The Cabbage was being nice. I was embarrassed. I didn't have the heart to ask her about sharing the horse.

There were posters up all over the walls at school. In two weeks the seventh grade Sadie Hawkins dance would be held on the day before February break. Girls would ask boys to be their date.

I was going to ask Steven Lancaster. It was part of my plan to become boyfriend and girlfriend. I figured if he went with me to the dance, he would see how great I was, and we would finally be a couple.

Steven was in my third hour skills for living class. I brought an invitation to give him. I needed to ask him to go with me as my date to Sadie's before anyone else had a chance to ask him. He would have to say yes.

I got to the room before anyone else. I put my books under my sewing machine and waited by the door. Kids were coming in. Where was Steven? Why was he late to class?

"Evan, have you seen Steven? Is he coming to class today?"

"No, Kate. He didn't come to school at all today. He's sick."

If I waited until Monday, every girl in school would ask him to the dance. I'd go to his house with some chicken soup and say I heard he was sick. I would give him the invitation I made. He'd surely want to go with me. I put Steven's invitation between the pages of my science lab book for safe-keeping.

I couldn't get the tie to go through the waistband of my pajama bottoms. I kept fumbling with it all hour. When the bell rang, I went to Miss Tibble's room for science class.

Elliot Einstein and I were working on our lab assignment. He did all the experiments, and I was in charge of recording the findings into both of our lab books, storing the supplies in our lab drawer and turning off the Bunsen burner.

"Kate. You have to wear your safety glasses. Remember, Miss Tibble always says, safety first. It is a rule. Please put them on," Elliot said. He was his usual nerdy, bossy self. "And tie your hair back."

"Okay," I said as I put my safety glasses on. I really didn't see the point in wearing the safety glasses when he wouldn't let me do anything but record our findings in the lab book. I tied my hair back with the hair tie I kept around my wrist.

After Miss Tibble sent me to the office in the

sixth grade to have my pants stapled, I couldn't stand her. How did I get so unlucky to have the meanest teacher two years in a row?

When Miss Tibble assigned lab partners, Elliot, the nerd, started quizzing me about scientific facts, just as he did in nursery school.

"Hey, Kate. Do you know how many legs a millipede has?"

"No, Elliot. I hate bugs. I would never look at a millipede, let alone count how many legs it has," I answered.

"Did you know that Albert Einstein is my distant relative?"

"No, Elliot. I never heard that before." It was only the millionth time he told me that fact since I first met him when we were three years old.

He probably was related to Albert. He sure looked smart with his slide rule and protractor in his pocket protector. We didn't use those tools anymore. Everyone had a scientific calculator to figure out the science and math problems.

This year's science class was easy. I sat there during the experiments and let Elliot do all the work. I wondered why Elliot was in the regular seventh grade science class and not the advanced science class with the rest of the seventh-grade nerds.

"Kate, remember, safety first," said Miss Tibble as she walked by checking to see if we were doing the experiments correctly.

I pretended to be doing something important.

"Of course, Miss Tibble, I am being very careful."

We were working with the Bunsen burners that day.

"Kate, don't touch the beakers. You might mix up the samples," said Elliot.

"Elliot, you have to let me do something."

"You are in charge of turning off the Bunsen burner at the end of class."

What was that saying? Righty-tighty, lefty-loosey?

"Kate, write down that the H2O reached the boiling point at 212 degrees Fahrenheit," Elliot demanded as he carefully removed the beaker from its place on the rack above the Bunsen burner.

I found the correct line to write the temperature in my book. I double checked between the pages. The invitation for Steven was still there. I then recorded the temperature in Elliot's book.

We finished the three experiments on boiling points. Monday we would be investigating and recording freezing points.

I was very hungry. I was in a hurry to go to lunch. I threw the supplies in the drawer we were assigned in the lab table. I gathered my books and made sure I didn't forget to put my science lab folder in my backpack.

Elliot was packing up his books and grabbed his lab book.

"Did you write my findings in my book, Kate?" he asked.

Elliot was concerned about his grades and doing everything right.

"Yes, Elliot. I recorded the findings, just like you told me. See you Monday," I said.

I felt like I was forgetting something. I looked through my stuff again. Everything was there.

On my way to the lunchroom, I had to stop in the lavatory to pee. I was the only kid in there. It smelled as bad as always. I plugged my nose. In the first stall there was pee all over the seat. Stall number two was plugged up with toilet paper and poop. I wasn't using that one.

The third stall was my only choice. I had to go so bad. I was almost going to pee my pants. I opened the door. Pee soup. The toilet was filled with pee and toilet paper, but the seat was clean. There was no way I would touch the handle with my bare hands. It was disgusting and full of germs. I raised my foot up in the air and pushed the handle with my black leather platform shoe. The toilet flushed.

I was still holding my nose. I lined the seat with six layers of toilet paper, and sat on the seat just in time. When I was done I wiped and stood up. I used my shoe to shove the toilet paper from the seat into the toilet. I was standing at an odd angle and holding my nose with one hand. when I lost my balance.

Before I could catch myself, my foot slipped

into the toilet and I was up to my ankle in swirling pee and toilet water. This couldn't be happening to me. I couldn't walk around all day with my shoe covered in pee! I really loved my platform shoes.

I got a wad of paper towels and used it to take off my wet shoe and sock. I threw my shoe, sock and the peed up paper towels in the garbage can. There was no other choice. I could never wear a shoe soaked in pee. Since I couldn't possibly hop around school on one foot, I had to take off my dry shoe and sock and throw them in the garbage, too. What would I tell my mom? She said those shoes were too expensive and I promised her I would wear them all year.

Last summer at camp was bad enough. When my shoe fell into the outhouse poop pit, I ended up wearing my flip-flops the whole week. Timmy and The Cabbage kept my secret, but Mom and Dad found out anyway. That was too embarrassing to repeat.

My athletic shoes were in my locker in the gym locker room. Somehow I had to go through the hallway and into the locker room without anyone noticing my bare feet. I peeked out the door of the lavatory. There was no one in the hall. The seventh graders were at lunch.

I went out the door and quickly made my way down the hall toward the gym. Some eighth graders were walking toward me. I couldn't take a chance of them noticing my bare feet. I sat on the floor and crossed my legs and put my books on my lap to hide my feet. Phew, they didn't seem to notice.

I got up and walked as fast as possible, remembering not to run in the halls on my way to the gym. I entered through the girls' side. It was very quiet in the locker room. There was a class playing basketball in the gym.

There were very strict rules about skipping class. I didn't have a hall pass. I should have been at lunch. I hoped no one would come in and catch me. I wasn't in the mood for an after-school detention.

I ducked around the corner and tiptoed to my gym locker. I quickly dialed the combination and opened the door. I found my gym socks and put them up to my nose to smell them. Thank goodness, they were not too stinky. I put them on and then put my gym shoes on. How would I explain my missing shoes to my mom?

I tip-toed through the locker room and carefully opened the door a crack and stuck my head out. The coast was clear. Lunch time was almost over. I waited until the bell rang, and before the gym class came into the locker room, I snuck out the door and filed into the hallway with the kids who were changing classes.

I went upstairs to my locker to get my books for the rest of the afternoon. If I wasn't so worried about what I was going to say to my mom about my missing shoes, I would have been thinking about how hungry I was from missing lunch. Every time my stomach growled, it reminded me of my shoes. I felt sick.

Just as I got my afternoon books out of my locker, the fire alarm sounded. The teachers came out of their classrooms to direct us calmly to the doors. There wasn't time to grab our coats.

In the case of a fire drill, we were to find our first hour class and meet in a designated area. I stood in line with the kids from my homeroom, Mr. Kulis's algebra class. Mr. Kulis walked over from the group of teachers he was talking to.

"Why do they always pick the coldest day of the year for a fire drill?" I asked Mr. Kulis as he took attendance.

As he checked off the students in his attendance book, Mr. Kulis said, "Kate, this time the fire alarm is real. It came from one of the science rooms. The fire trucks are on their way."

What? Oh, no. That's what I forgot.

"What science room is the fire in, Mr. Kulis?"

"In Miss Tibble's room, Kate."

Was I ever going to be in trouble! I didn't shut off the Bunsen burner! My heart was pounding in my chest.

A police car pulled up and drove over the grass. I could almost feel the hand cuffs around my wrists.

I heard the sirens wailing from down the road. Soon fire trucks were turning into the driveway where the buses usually lined up. The fire men jumped out of the trucks wearing their gear and unwinding the fire hoses from the trucks. Some firemen were carrying axes. They ran into the building.

Mr. Rodriguez walked in front of the waiting students. He climbed up and stood on the brick wall that surrounded the courtyard. He was holding a cordless microphone. Everyone stopped talking when Mr. Rodriguez said, "Attention, students of West Hills Middle School. There was a fire in Miss Tibble's science room. All the students have been accounted for with the morning attendance. Thank goodness, no one has been hurt."

I wasn't sure, but it seemed he was looking at me.

Mr. Rodriquez handed the microphone down to Mrs. Brown, his assistant principal. She was wearing a dress so she didn't climb on the wall.

"Students, the busses will be arriving within the next five minutes to take you home. They will be lined up at the back of the school. We expect you to remain calm and walk in single file lines to board the busses. The computer fan-out has started, and your parents are being notified that there will be an early dismissal today."

Mr. Rodriguez took the microphone back and said, "The fire chief has just notified me that the fire has been extinguished and it will be safe for you to return to school on Monday morning. You will not be allowed back into the building to gather your belongings from your lockers."

Some of the smart kids were complaining that they wouldn't be able to do their homework without their books. I was happy to leave my books in the locker and have no homework to do over the weekend. Thank goodness I had my science book with the invitation for Steven in my hand.

"Please wait with your homeroom teachers until all the busses are present," said Mr. Rodriguez.

A lot of kids were talking about the fire. No one was sure if it was started by someone or an accident. I must have turned off the Bunsen burner. No news was good news.

I looked down at my tennis shoes. I didn't have time to worry about the fire, my mom was going to kill me when she saw that I didn't have my platforms.

I ignored The Cabbage as she was walking toward her side door to go into her house. She asked, "Why are you coming to my house?"

"I need to talk to Aubra. Please go in and get her. I'll wait here."

"Why do you want to talk to my sister?" she asked.

"It's none of your business. Just tell her I'm waiting."

A few minutes later, Aubra came to the door. I could see The Cabbage lurking in their mudroom, trying to hear what I was about to say to her sister.

"Can I speak to you in private?"

Aubra stepped outside, closing the door behind

her.

"What's up?"

"You know my platform shoes?"

"What about them?"

"I sort of lost them and my mom is going to kill me. Can you take me to the mall tomorrow afternoon? I'll tell my mom you are helping me pick out a dress for our Sadie's dance."

"I'll take you if you help me pick a cute dress for the Sadie's dance at Lincoln High. Those shoes are very popular. A lot of girls at my school are wearing them," Aubra warned.

I hoped they still had a pair at the mall. If my mom found out I threw them away, she was going to kill me!

For services at Temple Saturday morning I wore some old boots I found in the back of my closet.

"Kate. Why are you wearing boots? It's not snowing. You should be wearing your school shoes," Mom commented when we got in the car to drive to the temple.

"My feet are cold," I answered as I climbed in the back seat with Timmy.

During services I couldn't think of anything but buying new shoes. When we got home, I asked mom if I could go to the mall with Aubra.

"Sure, Kate, I'm happy you're friends with Aubra. It is too bad you and Jo Ann haven't become friends again. You were so close at camp last summer."

"Mom, Jo Ann is mean. I will never be friends with her again."

After lunch Aubra honked her horn in front of my house. I ran out and jumped in the front seat. As I turned to put my seat belt on, I noticed The Cabbage was sitting in the back.

"Why are you here?" I asked.

I have to go to the mall, too," The Cabbage said.

This day couldn't get any worse. I had to pray there were some shoes like mine still on sale at the mall. I had to hope The Cabbage wouldn't tattle on me. She had such a big mouth.

We walked to the shoe department where mom and I bought the platform shoes.

"I am going to the dress shop on the second floor next to Macy's. Meet me there in thirty minutes," said Aubra.

The Cabbage was standing next to me.

"Why are you following me? Maybe you need someone with you to buy shoes but I can do this myself. Please go somewhere else," I said.

"You are so mean, Kate. I won't bother you. I'll sit on the chair while you shop," she said.

I walked around the store, looking at all the shoes. I found the display for my platform shoes. I picked up the shoe from the display and sat down on the other side of the store from The Cabbage.

"What can I get for you, Miss?" asked the tall, skinny kid who worked there.

"I need this shoe in a size eight in black leather."

"Sorry, miss. That was one of our most popular shoes this season. All we have left in the stock room is a size seven and a half in brown."

My mom would surely notice if I was wearing brown shoes. And how was I going wear shoes that were half-a-size too small? My size-eights were already a bit too tight.

"She'll take it," said The Cabbage.

"I will be right out. Do you need to try them on?" he asked.

"No, I guess I have no other choice," I replied.

I walked up to the cash stand to wait for him. The Cabbage was standing next to me again. She reached up and grabbed a can off the display wall in front of the cash register.

"We can put some of this black shoe polish on the shoes so your mom won't know they're brown," she said.

I didn't know what to say. The cashier had begun to ring up my purchase. "This must be your lucky day, young lady. These shoes are on sale. That will be seventy-four, ninety-five, plus tax," he said.

I pulled out my wallet and handed over the remainder of my babysitting money. After buying the skis last month, my bank account was nearly wiped out, and now I was buying a pair of shoes that were the wrong color and the wrong size.

"May I please borrow a few dollars?" I asked The Cabbage.

"Sure, Kate," she said as she handed me a five

dollar bill.

"You better throw in this shoe polish, too," I said as I handed the five to the sales man.

The Cabbage and I were silent as we walked through the mall to meet Aubra.

"What did you do this time, Kate? Where did you lose your shoes?" she asked.

"I didn't exactly lose them. I threw them out in the trash," I answered.

"Why? Didn't you like them anymore?"

"I actually loved them, but I sort of got my foot stuck in the toilet and I had to throw my shoe away. Then I had to throw the other one away."

"Pickle. You threw out your shoes again, just like at camp. You crack me up."

I laughed, too. "Thanks for going into the shoe store with me. I would never have thought of buying black shoe polish."

"When we get to my house, I'll help you change the color of your new shoes, then we will stretch them on my mom's shoe stretcher."

"You won't tell anyone, will you?"

"No, Kate. I won't tell," The Cabbage said.

"Cross your heart?"

She crossed her heart. It felt good having The Cabbage back as my friend.

Sunday afternoon, I took the pot of chicken soup left over from Friday night's dinner out of the fridge. I heated it up and ladled a generous portion into a disposable plastic container. Steven lived three streets over from us. I went to my room and opened up my lab book to get the invitation out.

The invitation wasn't there. The lab book I had in my room had Elliot Einstein's name written on the inside cover. I was in such a hurry to leave the science room on Friday, I had taken Elliot's lab book home with me by accident. That meant Elliot had my lab book and the invitation to the Sadie Hawkins Dance that I was going to give to Steven Lancaster, the cutest and most popular boy in West Hills Middle School. How was I going to get the invitation back from Elliot?

I threw the chicken soup down the kitchen sink and picked up the phone.

"Hello, Mrs. Einstein, this is Kate Baker. Is Elliot home?" I asked.

"Sure, Kate. Let me get him for you. "Elliot, Kate Baker is on the phone."

"Hi, Kate."

"I accidentally switched lab books with you, Elliot."

"I don't have your lab book. It's at school because of the fire drill."

Can we meet before first hour and switch them back?" I asked, hoping I could get the invitation before third hour and give it to Steven in our Skills for Living class.

"Sure, Kate, I'll give it to you tomorrow, but I won't be able to meet before school. I have to go to Dr. Tyler's office. Your mom is cleaning my teeth. I'll switch books with you in Science class."

I would see Steven in sewing class before Elliot

could give me the invitation. It would be too late.

"Elliot, don't look in my lab book before you give it to me."

"I won't Kate. I have to go now. I'm watching a special on the National Geographic channel about sea urchins."

"Okay. That will be great. Have fun at the dentist."

Monday morning couldn't come soon enough. The signs advertising the Sadie Hawkins dance were on every wall. It was a constant reminder that I had to get the invitation back from Elliot so I could give it to Steven.

Steven was sitting at his sewing machine working on his pajama pants. I walked over, and as usual, when I wanted to talk to him, I felt my face get hot and red.

"Steven, I have a letter to give you but it's in my lab book and I won't get it back until fourth hour. It is very important," I said. Why couldn't I just come out and ask him to go with me to Sadies? Why did I feel so nervous every time I talked to him It was my mom's fault for having us take baths together when we were babies. I wondered if he remembered that horrible embarrassment, too.

"Okay, Kate. Whatever. See if you can find me later today."

I went back to my sewing machine and worked all hour on the waistband of my pajama bottoms. My hands were still shaking from talking to Steven Lancaster, the most popular boy at West Hills

Middle School.

Fourth hour, when I got to science class, I looked around for signs of damage from the fire on Friday. There was some painting going on, but otherwise, the room looked pretty normal.

Elliot wasn't there yet. He got into class and sat next to me just as Miss Tibble was starting to talk. There was no way I could ask him to switch lab books while the teacher was making announcements.

"Class, as you know, there was a fire in our room on Friday. It originated from a Bunsen burner that was left on at station five," Miss Tibble said as she and everyone in the room looked toward Elliot and I.

"It is apparent the safety rules have not been followed. Elliot and Kate, please report to the office. Mrs. Brown is waiting to talk to you," Miss Tibble finished as she handed the hall pass to Elliot.

All the way to the office, Elliot didn't speak to me. I was shaking as I told the secretary that we were there to see Mrs. Brown.

"Elliot and Kate, please come in," Mrs. Brown said as she held her office door open.

"It seems as though you were careless and didn't shut off the Bunsen burner causing a fire and smoke damage to the science room. The school's insurance will cover the repairs that have to be done. Most of the work was finished over the weekend. Now we must find out who was responsible."

I opened my mouth to say it was my job to turn off the Bunsen burner. Before I had a chance, Elliot said, "I forgot to shut off the burner, Mrs. Brown. You can punish me any way you want. Kate did everything she was supposed to do."

"I am surprised, Elliot. You never have been in my office. I guess we will forgive you. Please be more careful in the future. This will not go on your record since you admitted your mistake. Thanks Elliot for being so forthcoming. You may both be excused. Go back to class," said Mrs. Brown.

Why was Elliot taking the blame? I kept my mouth shut. I didn't want to get into trouble. It wasn't so bad for Elliot. He was perfect. He never made mistakes.

We went back into the classroom quietly. Miss Tibble was lecturing about gases.

"Mr. Einstein and Miss Baker, welcome back to the class. You can get the notes you missed from your classmates," said Miss Tibble as she continued lecturing.

As we were leaving class to go to lunch, Elliot said, "Kate, I will go with you to Sadie's. Thanks for the invitation. By the way, Here is your lab book. Can you give me my lab book?

I handed Elliot his lab book along with my chance to go to Sadie's with Steven. I couldn't cancel going to the dance with Elliot since he took the blame for the fire.

Later that evening, after the Monday Night

School dinner, The Cabbage and I were sitting with Susan and Emily in the hallway when Elliot walked up.

"What are you wearing to the Sadies' Dance, Kate? My mom wants to know so she can buy you a matching corsage," asked Elliot.

"I don't know, let's talk about it later," I said under my breath.

"Let me know," he said. "I have to go to practice my haftorah with Mr. Levine."

I didn't want Susan and Emily to hear I was going to the Sadie Hawkins Dance with Elliot, The Nerd, Einstein. It would be hard to hide this tid-bit of information, but I wanted to hide it as long as possible.

"Aren't you going with your boyfriend Steven Lancaster? I thought you do all kinds of fun things together?" asked Susan.

"Kate decided Elliot is cooler than Steven," The Cabbage chimed in.

Since Saturday afternoon when she helped me stretch and change the color of my too-small shoes, The Cabbage was being very nice to me.

"I have never seen Steven Lancaster, but the girls at East Hills talk about how cute he is all the time," said Emily.

"He looks okay, but I was getting tired of him talking about sports all the time," I lied. the truth was, Steven Lancaster never talked to me. True, he was hot, but he spent more time looking at himself in the mirror than looking at all the girls who were swooning over him.

Elliot was kind of good-looking, in a funny sort of way, I thought. It must have been the way he saved me from getting in trouble today for nearly burning down the science room. Elliot Einstein was growing on me.

On Friday, the day of the Sadies dance, I woke up, walked into my bathroom and threw up all over the floor. It felt like the room was spinning around me when I was sitting still.

The one time I really wanted to go to school, I was too sick to get out of bed. Mom left a message at Elliot's house that I wouldn't be going to the dance, since I had the flu.

The next week was winter break. The stomach flu turned into a cough and bronchitis. The doctor said I couldn't go to the stable and had to stay home and rest.

Wednesday morning, the phone rang while I was laying in bed. Timmy brought it to me with oven mits. He didn't want to get sick and ruin his break from school.

"Hi Kate. How are you?"asked the Cabbage.

"Not too good," I sniffled. "How did the dance go?"

"I didn't go and neither did Elliot. We both said it wouldn't be fun without you. I am not going anywhere for break. I'll be taking care of King this week. Try to convince your parents to let you share him with me. You get better. I'll see you when school starts up in March," said The Cabbage.

It felt good to have my best friend back. I spent the rest of the week off coughing, blowing my nose and convincing Mom and Dad that having half-a-horse was better than none. They said they would discuss it and get back to me.

CHAPTER 7
MARCH TO A DIFFERENT DRUMMER

Kate's Mom and Dad agreed that sharing King with me made more sense than her continuing on with gymnastics.

"The doctor said riding horses won't be as harmful to Kate's back as walkovers and round-offs," said Mrs. Baker when she stopped over on Sunday morning to have coffee with my mom.

"Tuesday and Thursday after school and Saturday afternoons will be my turn for going to the stables to take care of King. Your mom said you will do Monday, Wednesday and Friday and we can go together on Sundays. Our parents are going to split the costs," said Kate when she surprised me by ringing the doorbell early Monday morning before the other bus-stop kids arrived.

"Let's go to the stable together tomorrow. We need to practice our song for the Spring Musical and I have an idea for our Make a Difference project," said Kate on Friday after school.

"What's your idea?" I asked Kate as we mucked out King's stall.

"You know how I bring a wheeling suitcase to school? I think all the kids have sore backs from carrying all their books."

"I know my back kills sometimes, too," I said.

Aubra picked us up from the stable and we stopped at the office supply store to buy posters and markers.

We went to my house to work on our project. We practiced our duet for the Spring Musical as we drew the posters.

"I think we should use a turtle for our logo. Aubra told me you looked like an upside-down turtle when you fell over on top of your backpack." I thought Kate would be angry with me. I wasn't supposed to know about Aubra saving her that day back in October.

"That sounds like a great idea," said Kate.

We made twenty posters to put up all over school.

DOES YOUR BACK HURT?
LEAVE YOUR
BACKPACK AT HOME.
WHEEL YOUR BOOKS IN A
SUITCASE ON WHEELS.
NO MORE ACHING BACKS!

KATE AND JO ANN'S
MAKE A DIFFERENCE PROJECT

"Can you come with me to babysit tonight? We can share the money when Mrs. Cohen pays me. The kids like you and it is more fun to have someone with me when I sit. It gets boring waiting for them to come home."

"Sure. It sounds like fun," I answered.

On Sunday we went to the stables together and rode King and Jersey. Afterwards, we went back to my house to fill out the Make a Difference project form.

"I'm excited to finally turn in our project idea in Social Studies. We won't have an incomplete anymore," I said.

"Who is that a picture of?" Kate asked, pointing at a picture frame in our family room.

"That's my dad," I answered.

"Wow, he looks familiar," said Kate.

"You know, he died when I was three and I still miss him."

Monday couldn't come too soon. Kate's mom drove us to school. We had our posters to carry, and I now was wheeling a suitcase with my books, too.

"Not a bad idea for a project. We will be saving the sacroiliacs of all of the kids at West Hills Middle School!" Kate exclaimed.

"Turtle Force!" we said at the same time.

When we got in school, we taped our posters up in every hallway. We went to our homerooms and later we met for lunch.

"You girls finally have your project handed in. I saw the posters all over the school. Very good job," said Miss Jenkins.

At Monday Night School we told Emily and Susan about our Make a Difference project.

"That's an amazing idea. My back is always sore from carrying heavy books," said Susan.

"Mine, too," said Emily.

Tuesday morning everyone at the bus stop had wheeling suitcases. The aisle of the bus was filled with suitcases. We had to climb over them to sit in the seats.

"This is a safety hazard," said the bus driver as we wheeled our suitcases off the bus.

"It is a safety hazard for us to carry such heavy backpacks," Kate said.

When we got to school, kids were pulling wheeling suitcases up the stairs. There were suitcases lined up and down the hallway in front of every locker.

"Jo Ann. Great idea!" said Jennifer, an eighth grader who had a horse boarded at the stable. She was wheeling a faux leopard-print suitcase toward her locker.

When we got to social studies, Miss Jenkins called us up to her desk. "Kate and Jo Ann, Mr. Rodriguez wants to see you in his office. Here's a hall pass."

"Mr. Rodriguez probably wants to congratulate us for our great idea," said Kate.

"We arc here to see the principal," I said to the

secretary.

"He will be with you in a minute. Please sit there and wait," she said pointing to the chairs against the wall.

"Miss Elkavich and Miss Baker, please come in," said Mr. Rodriguez.

We walked in and sat in the two chairs facing his desk.

"There seems to be quite an uproar throughout the school. You have made an impression on everyone in only one day!"

I looked at Kate. She was smiling proudly. I felt very proud, too.

"The phone has been ringing off the hook. The bus drivers are concerned for the safety of the students on the bus. The teachers' union called and said there is a horrible safety issue since the teachers could trip over suitcases lined up and down the hallways."

"Are you serious? What about the students' backs? Don't you care? I had to stop gymnastics because my back hurts so bad from carrying tons of books every day," said Kate.

"All the kid's parents went out and bought them suitcases to wheel their books in. What about that? They are happy," I said.

"Too bad. Your project is over. I usually leave these matters up to Mrs. Brown, your vice-principal, but due to the urgency of this matter, I will be making an announcement over the public address system in a few minutes. I will also send out an e-mail to all the parents. Suitcases with wheels are banned at West Hills Middle School and all schools in the district."

We went back to Miss Jenkins' classroom. We sat in our seats as Mr. Rodriguez made his announcement.

"Girls, I will expect you to have a new project by the end of the week," Miss Jenkins said in front of the entire class. "You may leave early to remove the posters from the hallways."

We tore down the posters. The turtle looked sad. On the way to the bus kids stopped us to say thanks for trying to help.

The bus driver smirked, "I told you the suitcases were a safety hazard."

We wheeled our suitcases toward my front door.

"We'll come up with another idea," said Kate. "I am going home. I have to go to the stable."

"I don't know if it will be by the end of the week. I am all out of ideas," I replied.

On Thursday night Kate and I got together to brainstorm.

"What if we clean up the river?" asked Kate.

"Another group is doing that," I said. "We need something original.

Aubra walked into my room. "What are you two doing?"

"We are trying to come up with a new Make a Difference project.

"You already had a great idea. Is there any way

you could go to the television stations or go on the Web and make your case? The schools have been killing our backs with heavy books for years. Something has to be done!" exclaimed Aubra. My sister usually didn't get involved in my problems.

Kate picked up the picture of my dad that I kept on my dresser.

"He looks so familiar. I can't be sure, since it was back in December, but a man came our door saying he was a census taker. He looked like your dad in this picture. He asked me questions about your family. I told him your mom lived alone with you and Aubra. Then I saw a commercial saying Census takers won't ask about other people," said Kate.

"I saw a suspicious car parked on the street. When I walked toward it, it drove away," said Aubra.

"I have been hearing odd sounds in the middle of the night. I looked outside and saw a man walking down the street. Who walks around at three in the morning?" I said. "Someone has been calling and hanging up, too.

"It is probably our imaginations," said Aubra. There are a lot of handsome men who look like dad. Don't worry, Kate. You didn't do anything wrong. The Census taker was probably lost. Our dad passed away nine years ago. We have over-active imaginations."

"Let's watch television. Maybe it will give us some ideas for our project," I said as I hit the button on the remote.

"The petition to add Mark Smith to the ballot was a success," said the news reporter.

"That is a great idea, Kate," I said. "We should start a petition to change the policy about backpacks."

"Do you have the scale, Kate?" I asked.

"Yes, do you have the petition?" Kate asked.

"Yes. Let's do it," I said.

Kate's dad drove us to school early. We set up our things at the door where the kids came in from their busses. I had each person put their backpack on the scale and wrote down the weight. Kate had them sign the petition saying they were tired of having aching backs from carrying heavy backpacks.

In Social Studies, we asked Miss Jenkins for an extension on our Make a Difference project.

"I don't know what your girls are up to. It better be good. The suitcases didn't work out. It caused quite an uproar. Jo Ann, please read me your petition," Miss Jenkins said.

"I do hear-by swear that my backpack is too heavy and my back often hurts. Something has to be done to lighten the load of books we carry to and from school."

"Sounds good. What do you plan to do after you gather the rest of the signatures?" Miss Jenkins asked.

"We aren't sure, yet," said Kate.

"We will let you know when we know," I said.

Every morning that week we went to school early. We weighed backpacks and had kids read and sign the petition. The only kid who didn't carry a heavy backpack was Elliot Einstein.

"Where are your books, Elliot?" I asked.

"I don't bring them to school," Elliot replied as he signed the petition.

I didn't have time to ask him why he left his books at home. There were other students waiting to sign the petitions.

By Thursday we had 500 signatures. On Friday we waited by the parent drop-off door and got the remaining 100 students to sign the petition.

After I got home from the stable I brought my laptop to Kate's house. We recorded the weights of the backpacks on my computer. The average weight of the backpacks was 19.8 pounds. Kate called her doctor on the phone. I listened on the speaker-phone.

"Do you think 19.8 pounds is too much for a middle school student to carry on their back?" she asked.

"Yes. It is too much for a middle school student, or for anyone to carry," he said.

We entered the doctor's expert opinion on our report.

"We know the school won't let us bring rolling suitcases for our books. Do you think they would let us leave the books at school?" I asked Kate.

Monday morning we had my mom drop us off

at school early. Kate and I went to the principal's office. We were fired up and ready to make our case.

"I am sorry, girls. Mr. Rodriguez is in meetings all week. You will have to come back next Monday. I'll give you an appointment," said the secretary.

We left the office and went to our homerooms before the bell rang. On the way to second hour choir class I had to go to the restroom something awful.

As I was going into the girl's lavatory on the second floor, Mallory and Kelsey were leaving. They were laughing hysterically. I didn't know them well, but from what I had seen since I started at West Hills, I knew I didn't like them.

The first thing I saw was a huge sign written on the mirror in bright pink lipstick, "Kate Baker Poops Her Pants." I couldn't prove it, but I bet Mallory and Kelsey had something to do with it.

Other girls who had followed me in to use the washroom read the horrible pink message and started laughing. They were making fun of my best friend, Kate.

I ripped off a long piece of paper toweling and wiped the incriminating message off the mirror. I folded up the paper and put it in my pocket.

I went to choir class and sat down next to Kate. Mr. Balbes was sitting at the piano playing the scales so the class could warm up their vocal chords.

I whispered to Kate, "Do you know anyone who

wears bright pink lipstick?" I pulled out the paper towel and showed her.

"No, I don't. Why?"

"Jo Ann and Kate would you like to share your secret with the rest of the class?" Mr. Balbes asked.

"No, sir. We would like to sing our duet for the class if you don't mind," I answered.

Before Kate sang the first note I whispered, "I will tell you later," and we began to sing.

The following Monday morning Kate and I went to meet with Mr. Rodriguez.

"Okay, girls. What is your new idea for the Make a Difference project?"

We showed the principal our petitions.

"One hundred percent of the students at West Hills, minus Elliot Einstein, find carrying heavy packs painful. My doctor said the average weight of the bags is dangerous to all of our backs," said Kate.

"Would it be possible for students to leave books in the classrooms and not have to carry them back and forth?" I asked.

"Textbooks are a necessary tool in the classroom. The teachers base assignments on the material in the textbooks. Asking students what they want will not get you anywhere. You have to ask the teachers."

Kate and I made a new questionnaire to give the teachers. We brought it in the next day. As we were putting one in each teacher's mailbox, the secretary stopped us.

"What do you girls think you're doing? The teachers don't like getting paper mail. They feel it's a waste of natural resources to have unnecessary junk mail put in their boxes. You need to contact them via Email."

We gathered up the notices and left the office.

After school we went through the website and sent our questionnaire out to all the teacher's Emails.

A few days later we started receiving replies. Every teacher except Mr. Balbes said they believed in textbooks and there was no other way to teach and learn.

Mr. Balbes replied that so much of music was theory. Although the school board required him to assign books to all his students, he preferred to teach us himself.

"I can't believe the counselor once left me a note in my locker to come to her office. And how about all of the handouts the teachers give us? If teachers insist on saving paper, why do they make us carry around books and workbooks?" Kate asked.

"Well, I guess it's back to the drawing board," I said.

There wasn't time to tell Miss Jenkins we still didn't have a Make a Difference project. The entire seventh grade was going on a full day Urban Field Trip to the city of Detroit. We spent the next week discussing the history of the city and the rules we had to follow on the trip.

Spring had sprung. The only snow remaining was that dirty, black snow on the edge of the curbs and some tall mountains of filthy snow in the middle of parking lots.

Granny called the previous night to tell us the snow in the Upper Peninsula was waist high. A shorter winter was one advantage to moving down-state. Living in our own house with my mom and Aubra was another. Being friends with Kate was the best advantage.

The day of the Urban Field Trip finally arrived. The busses let us out in the bus circle. We each brought our empty backpack with a sack lunch. The school was providing drinks. It was the lightest my backpack had ever been.

I went to find Mr. Spangler, my homeroom teacher, and our class. The yellow school busses drove away, and in their place were four long, shiny motor coaches.

There was a bathroom at the back of the bus. It smelled like the outhouses at camp. I breathed through the collar of my jacket so I wouldn't have to breathe it in. I noticed Kate was doing the same thing a couple rows ahead.

Mr. Spangler stood at the front of the bus with Mr. Kulis. He held a microphone to make an announcement. " Students, since we are going into the big city, we need to use a buddy system so no one gets lost. You will be partnered up with the person in the seat next to you."

I was sitting next to Elliot. He had become a

great friend during Monday Night School. Kate never told me why she suddenly tolerated Elliot, and to tell the truth, I never asked her.

I noticed Kate was sitting alone. I raised my hand.

"Miss Elkavich, do you have a question?" asked Mr. Kulis.

"Yes. I noticed Kate Baker is by herself. Would it be okay if she joined Elliot and I in our buddy group?"

"Miss Elkavich. You and Mr. Einstein may team up with Miss Baker," said Mr. Spangler.

Kate turned around and gave me the thumbs-up.

We reached our first destination, the Detroit Institute of Arts.

"Hey, Kate do you have to go?" I asked pointing at the lady's room.

"No. Not at this time. I'll wait with Elliot."

When I entered the fancy marble bathroom, Mallory was standing at the mirror putting on lipstick.

"Mallory, that's an interesting color of pink. I wonder if it matches the color of lipstick I have been wanting from the store?

"I don't know, Jo Ann, would you like to try it on?"

"Sure," I said as I reached out for the lipstick tube.

I took out the paper towel from my pocket. I had been carrying it around ever since the 'Lipstick

Incident' in the school lavatory.

"I don't have cooties. You don't have to wipe it off," said Mallory.

"This is exactly the same color as the lipstick I found on the mirror in the girl's room in school."

"Hey, Jo Ann, what's taking so long? We are ready to go into the museum," said Kate as she stuck her head in the door.

"I think you have some explaining to do, Mallory."

I motioned to Kate and she walked in.

"Mallory why did you write bad things on the mirror about my friend?" I asked pointing toward Kate. "And where is Kelsey, your follower?"

"She was sick today and couldn't come on the field trip. I didn't write that Kate poops her pants."

"I believe you did, Mallory. You have been teasing me about what happened in kindergarten for the past seven years," said Kate.

"You better stop bullying Kate. She is my best friend and I won't allow it," I said.

"I'm sorry. I won't do it again, I promise. I am alone today. They didn't pair me up with anyone since Kelsey isn't here," said Mallory.

"Would you like to be in our group?" asked Kate.

"That sounds great. I am truly sorry. I won't do it again."

Mallory walked out with us. Elliot was waiting by the entrance to the Diego Rivera gallery.

"I already looked at all the murals. I have a

photographic memory. You don't even have to go in there. I can tell you what each one looks like in detail."

"Wow, Elliot. Is that why you don't carry a huge, heavy backpack to school?" asked Kate.

"Yes. Once I speed-read an assignment, I never forget it."

"You speed-read? How do you do that?" I asked.

"I took a course a few years ago at my Mensa Club."

Kate was right. Elliot was a bit weird. In a good way.

After the museum, our two homerooms went on a walking tour of the neighborhood. There was a century-old house being renovated. Mr. Spangler and Mr. Kulis told us after touring the house to meet on the front porch in thirty minutes.

Before we went in the house I noticed a dog walking down the street.

"Oh, look how cute he is," I said.

"There are a lot of stray dogs in the city. If you come upon any, don't feed them or pet them," said Mr. Kulis. Sometimes they bite.

There wasn't much to see in the house. The furniture was similar to what we had in our house. We finished looking at the house in about ten minutes.

We had twenty minutes left-over. The four of us went out the back door and into the alley. I heard a muffled cry. Stuck behind the dumpster was a tiny puppy. I picked him up. There was no sign of a mother dog.

"He's so cute," said Mallory.

"He looks like my Bubby's old Schnauzer," Kate said.

"You probably shouldn't touch him. He may have parasites," said the worry-wart, Elliot. And Mr. Kulis said you could get bitten!

I took out my lunch from my backpack and picked a few pieces of chicken out of my sandwich. The puppy gobbled each morsel and kept wanting more. His little teeth barely hurt as he nibbled the little pieces of food from my fingers.

After the chicken was gone I put the puppy on the ground, and he pooped and peed. I picked him up and he promptly fell asleep in my arms.

"I'm keeping him. He needs a home."

"What are you going to name him, Jo Ann?" asked Kate.

"I'm going to call him Motown, Mo for short."

"He may have fleas or ticks!" Elliot was always concerned about insects.

We caught up with the others in our group. We walked to the Wayne State University Student Union to eat lunch. Everyone was so interested in the tour. No one noticed I was carrying Mo under my jacket. As we walked through the door, I slipped the sleeping dog into my backpack.

On the way home Mallory got permission from her homeroom teacher to come on our bus. Kate sat with me and Elliot sat with Mallory. Mallory wasn't so bad when Kelsey wasn't with her. Some girls were mean in groups. It's hard to be mean when you were alone.

"Your mom won't mind you bringing Mo home with you?" Kate asked.

"No. When we moved here we had to leave all our pets at Granny's house. Mom was talking about us getting a dog. She'll be fine with it."

I unzipped the bag part way. We both reached in and petted little Motown. He was waking up from his long nap when we arrived at West Hills.

Mom was waiting to drive Elliot, Kate and I home. I was going to show her Motown when we arrived at our house. Once she saw him, she would love him.

As we walked toward the minivan, I noticed a man driving out of the parking lot. He looked very familiar. He looked like my dad.

CHAPTER 8
PANTING AND PIDDLING

Motown was covered with fleas. He needed a bath the minute Jo Ann took him out of her backpack. Her mom wasn't totally happy with her bringing a dog home from the inner city, but she let her keep him.

"I promised my mom I would take care of Mo. He piddles on the floor about half the time. The other half he goes outside. He's learning," Jo Ann said when I came to her house on Monday morning before the bus.

I will never understand girls. Kate was plucking Jo Ann's eyebrows. I could see tears in her eyes.

"Elliot, you have a bit of a uni-brow going on. Do you want me to pluck your eyebrows?" Kate asked.

"No, not right now. It's getting late. The bus will be here in a few minutes." The guys at school already made fun of me. If they heard I was getting groomed by the girls, I would never hear the end of it.

"My mom said she has had it with Izzy and Lizzy pooping all over the family room. We are going to give them to the zoo," Kate announced since we were talking about pets.

"We'll have King for another three months, then Uncle Tom will take him up to Camp Anishinabe for the summer," Jo Ann said.

"I'm starting gymnastics on Tuesdays and Thursdays again. The doctor said I can give it a try. Hopefully my back won't hurt. I'll need to change stable days with you," said Kate.

"Can we get a day together at the stables? You know how you said you saw a man who looks like my dad? I saw a guy in the school parking lot who looked like him, too," said Jo Ann.

She continued, "We should ride horses to the air base. It isn't too far from the stable. I want to sneak in and check out their records. The story was that Dad disappeared on a Top Secret mission. They never found his body, but declared him dead. I have to see for myself that my dad really did die in Afghanistan,"

Girls sure talk fast.

"Have you told your mom you that we all think we saw someone who looked like your dad?" Kate asked.

"Every time I talk about him, she gets upset. I want to be sure before I say anything to Mom," Jo Ann said as she wiped a tear from her eye.

"Elliot can you come with us? You have a photographic memory. You will be able to speed-read the file and memorize it. It will make our job much easier."

"Okay, Kate. I'll go to the stable with you and Jo Ann. I can't go on Thursdays since I have my Mensa meeting," I said.

"Is that the genius club you go to?" asked Jo Ann.

"I guess you can call it that. I'll think up a plan."

"If anyone can come up with a plan, it's you, Elliot," said Kate.

I could feel myself blushing.

"I can carry a heavy backpack. I am strong," Steven Lancaster said as he pulled down a poster that Kate and Jo Ann put up for their Make a Difference project.

"Hey, don't pull that off the wall," I said.

"I'm a star football player and wrestler. What do you do Einstein? Lift a slide rule? You're so weak, you don't even carry a backpack," Steven said as he shoved me.

"I have a photographic memory. I speed-read the books and leave them at home." I said.

"Have you seen Kate staring at me? She thinks I like her. She is too skinny and tall. Not my type. I heard she wanted to go with me to the Sadie's dance. There was no way I would go with her."

"She didn't go to the dance. She was sick."

"I would rather be strong than smart," said Steven Lancaster. He shoved me again.

I used a move I learned from a karate video and I grabbed him by the arm and pulled it behind him. He fell to the ground.

"Einstein, I saw that. Come with me to the office," said the coach.

"I saw you take Lancaster down. I know he has been a bully forever. I didn't know you had it in you, Einstein. You should join the wrestling team. Come in after school tomorrow for practice," the coach said as we walked past the Principal's office.

"So I don't have to go to the Principal, Coach?"

"No, Elliot, just show up at practice."

Before Miss Tibble got into the Science Class on Thursday, Kate asked me, "would you be able to come to the stable with Jo Ann and I after school tomorrow?"

"That sounds cool, Kate. It's lucky you don't want me to come today. I am starting wrestling team after school."

"I thought you had Mensa Club on Thursdays."

"I cancelled it. We were going to debate Newton's theory that the gravitational field will bend when a beam of light is shined around the sun. Albert Einstein said time would stand still as the continuum goes forward..."

I could tell that Kate didn't understand a word I said. She looked at me with a blank look. That happened a lot when I talked about my hero, Albert Einstein.

I was still talking when Miss Tibble stood in front of the room to start class.

"Elliot, please be quiet. I am surprised that you are not ready for class to start," said Miss Tibble.

I hoped we weren't making a mistake going on the mission. If we did get the answers Jo Ann wanted, those answers may be more than she could handle.

After school I went into the boy's locker room

to suit up for wrestling practice. I pulled the one-piece, skin-tight wrestling uniform on over my shorts. I felt like I had an atomic wedgy! I put the helmet on and walked into the gym.

"Hey, look at Einstein, he has the helmet on backwards," laughed Steven Lancaster.

The other guys started to laugh, too.

I took the helmet off and turned it the right way.

Coach came in and went over the rules of the wrestling match. We divided up into teams.

"Einstein, you will go up against Lancaster. Your heights are a match and you weigh almost the same."

Coach started the timer. I calculated Steven's every move. The bell rang for the first period. Before I knew it, I took him down to the mat and bested him in all three periods.

"Einstein, good job. We're glad to have you on our team."

"Thanks, Coach. I'm glad, too."

I went into the locker room to change.

"I have to admit, Einstein. I didn't play to my full potential today. I let you win."

"Right, Steven. Think what you want, but I am coming back."

Friday after school Jo Ann's sister, Aubra, picked me up. I was wearing the cowboy outfit and red bandana my mom bought me. I noticed the girls giggling when I walked toward Aubra's car. They stopped when I got in.

"We're going for a ride around the trails. Can you pick us up at six?" Kate asked Aubra.

"Sure. Not any later, though. I have plans tonight," Aubra said.

"Okay, six it is," said Jo Ann.

I made a map on my tablet. We needed to go through the neighborhoods and woods to avoid the main roads as much as possible so we wouldn't arouse too much suspicion on our way to the air base.

The first problem was, I wasn't sure we could get there and back in two hours. The second problem was, I had never ridden a horse before.

"Elliot. Can you take off that cowboy hat? It will surely attract attention," Jo Ann said.

"I am going to wear my hat. It looks good," I said.

"Okay. If you want to wear it, go ahead," Jo Ann said.

"Now, Elliot, put your left foot in this stirrup and pull your right leg over the saddle and sit on it," said Kate as she demonstrated how to get on the horse.

"Use the saddle horn to hold on to while you pull yourself over," said Jo Ann.

I did what they said and somehow I ended up backwards in the saddle. Kate and Jo Ann were laughing hysterically. I didn't think it was funny. I was very high off the ground. If I fell I would break my head open.

I slid off the horse. I tried again, putting my left

foot in the stirrup and pulling my right foot up and over the horses back. Before I could stop myself, I was upside-down under the horse's belly. My cowboy hat was laying on the ground next to me. Once again, the girls were laughing uncontrollably.

"Hey, I have never done this before. Give me one more chance," I said as I walked over and hung my hat on a nail sticking out of the wall.

The third time was a charm. I was perched high above the ground, sitting on the horse's back, like a real cowboy, ready to ride. I held the bridle and kicked the sides of the horse.

"Giddy-up, horsey," I said. The horse actually started to move in the same direction as Kate and Jo Ann's horses. We were on our way.

As we rode along I told the girls my plan. I had studied a diagram of the air base on a satellite website. I memorized the entrances and exits.

"I have calculated how fast a horse can trot. It should take exactly 45 minutes to ride there." The problem was, it was taking longer since the ground was still muddy from the snow melting. When we finally got to the air base, it was 5:15.

We dismounted and tied the horses to a near-by grove of bushes. There wasn't much cover. Planes can't take off and land around a lot of tall trees.

"According to my plan, Kate, you need to distract the guard while Jo Ann and I get through the gate. We will then go into the building where they keep the records."

"What will I say to the guard?" Kate asked.

"Tell him you are here for an air show. If he challenges you, tell him you are sure this is the day. Keep him busy while we sneak by," said Jo Ann.

Kate started talking to the guard. He seemed to be very helpful. While kept him distracted, Jo Ann and I slipped by and ran behind the mess hall and into the Records Office. Amazingly, the door wasn't locked.

Since it was late in the afternoon, the office workers weren't in the building. Jo Ann and I walked across the room to a wall of file cabinets. There was one marked "E" on the front. She opened the drawer and pulled it out. There were hundreds of files, each with a name on the tab. One was labeled "Elkavich, Diane"

"Hey, that's my mom's file," said Jo Ann."

Right behind it was a file labeled, "Eric Elkavich."

"That's my dad," said Jo Ann with a gasp.

Just as she pulled the file from the drawer, the door opened and in walked the guard with Kate. Jo Ann pushed the file back into the drawer. Without anyone noticing, I grabbed it and stuffed it in the back of my shirt.

"What do you think you are doing?" asked the guard. He didn't look too happy.

"Isn't this the library?" asked Jo Ann, looking as innocent as possible.

"No, of course not. You have to leave

immediately," said the guard.

"Oh, our mistake," I said.

The guard escorted us out the door and toward the gate.

"Don't come back here. These files are the property of the United States Air Force."

"We have our rights. We are citizens," said Kate.

"Tell it to your congressman," the guard said. He turned around and picked up a phone.

I was sure the military police or some other police were going to catch us and put us under arrest. We left as quickly as possible, ran to the horses and rode back toward the stables. I kept looking back. No one was following us.

"Did you see? I had my dad's file in my hands. I didn't have time to open it. What am I going to do, now?" asked Jo Ann. She started to cry. I hated to see a girl cry.

"That's okay, Cabbage. You did your best. I am sure you'll find out what happened to your dad," said Kate.

"I guess it wasn't meant to be. I will never be sure," Jo Ann said.

"I think I slowed you down. I am not a good rider. It took so long to get there. The plan didn't go down the way it was supposed to."

"Elliot, you did the best you could. I am grateful we saw his name on his file."

It seemed to take forever to get back to the stable. I didn't tell the girls I had the file. I wanted to read it by myself in case there was any information in it that would hurt Jo Ann and her family.

It was way after seven when we got back. Aubra was waiting in the corral. She had her arms crossed and was tapping her foot angrily against the dirt. Mrs. Elkavich and Mrs. Baker were there, too.

"Where have you been? You are one hour late. Mr. Smith came to ride Jersey and you had him out. He went looking for you in his car. He saw you riding over by the air base.

"Why did you go so far and for over three hours? You can't take someone else's horse out without permission," said Mrs. Elkavich.

"Kate you have to lose your privileges with the horses for a while. You will just come, muck the stables, exercise the horses for a short time and come home. Separately. For two weeks," said Mrs. Baker.

"It's my fault, Mrs. Baker and Mrs. Elkavich. I wanted to learn to ride. It was so much fun, I kept telling the girls to go a bit further. They wanted me to have a good time."

"It doesn't matter, Elliot. The girls know the rules," said Mrs. Elkavich.

"Let's go. I'm late for my date," said Aubra.

When I got home I went straight to my room.

"Elliot, did you have a good time riding the horse?" my mom yelled up from the kitchen.

"Yes, Mom. I had a great time."

Dinner would be soon, but I wanted to get a look at Mr. Elkavichs' file. I opened the manila folder. Inside was a white sheet of paper. On it there was a huge red stamp.

TOP SECRET

I was disappointed. There were no other pages. There was no reason to upset Jo Ann until I had more time to investigate.

The next time I saw the girls together was at the bus stop on Monday.

"We won't be going back to the air base again," said Jo Ann. "My mom figured out why we went there, and she said I have to drop the subject. My dad died in Afghanistan, and I have to stop coming up with conspiracy theories."

"I had everything planned on my tablet. It should have worked." I said nothing about the manila file.

"Why would you need the tablet? I thought you memorized everything," asked Kate.

"I scan my textbooks and assignments into my tablet. Then I speed read it all and take notes on the tablet," I explained.

"Are you thinking what I am thinking, Kate," said Jo Ann.

"Yes, I think I am, Cabbage. We should be reading all of our textbooks on tablets. We wouldn't have to carry as much in our backpacks. Just a tablet and a few notebooks," said Kate.

"You did a great thing trying to help us, Elliot. We may need your super-powers again, some day," said Jo Ann.

"Thanks for trying to take the blame with our mom's, too." said Kate.

"Come to the wrestling meet and see me use my super powers," I said.

"We will be there," replied Jo Ann and Kate simultaneously.

On the second night of Passover my mom invited the Elkavich and Baker families for dinner. We crowded around the dining room table and gorged ourselves on matzo ball soup, brisket and all kinds of desserts.

We read through the Hagadah, with Kate's little brother, Timmy answering the Four Questions.

It bothered me that I had not told Jo Ann about the manila folder. I had done some research on the folder from the air base.

After dinner the kids went down to the basement to play pool. Aubra stayed upstairs to help with the dishes.

"Timmy, I have this cool video game I programmed. would you like to play it?"

"Sure Elliot," Timmy said as I turned on the game and walked over to the pool table where Jo Ann and Kate were racking the balls.

My older brother, Ethan, was away at college. He used to have the basement bedroom, but when he went away to college, my mom and dad said I could make it my laboratory.

"Jo Ann, I didn't want to tell you until I did some research, but I snuck your dad's file from the airbase. I hope you aren't angry with me," I said quietly.

"No, I'm not mad. What did you find out?" she asked as she and Kate came closer to hear me.

I looked over at Timmy. He was busy playing my video game.

"Through my research I found out that when an airman is missing in action, they remove all vital information and put a Top Secret notice in his record. They don't close the case until they find him.

Sometimes they do the same thing when he dies in action. I am sorry, Jo Ann. I wish I had a better answer for you."

"Thanks, Elliot. You did your best," said Jo Ann.

CHAPTER 9
MAY WE HAVE YOUR ATTENTION?

I was very disappointed with the trip to the air base last month. I was sure we would have found answers about my dad. My mom basically closed all doors that night when we came back from the stable by saying, "you aren't to go back to the air base. I know why you went. You are curious about your dad. He is gone. We have gotten along all these years without him and we will be okay."

When I fell asleep, I dreamt my dad and I were flying in a small, single-engine plane. The plane started spiraling out of control. We were coming close to crashing when my seat ejected me out of the plane. I drifted down on a soft cloud. I was okay, but my dad was still in the plane when it plummeted to the ground with a loud crash. Pages and pages of white paper came down from the sky. Each one had a huge red stamp on it saying, 'Top Secret!'

I woke crying. I stood up on my bed and ripped the dreamcatcher from the wall. It wasn't working. Sad dreams still came, and a piece of wood with feathers hanging from it was not banishing the bad thoughts from my mind. Only answers could do that.

Why did I think I saw my dad at the school? Why did Kate see a man who looked like my dad's picture? If Dad was alive, why wouldn't he want to see me?

"Are you sure you girls don't want to change your project? This is your last chance. If you aren't successful, you will both get an incomplete in Social Studies. I am sorry to say, you will both have to repeat the seventh grade," Miss Jenkins said when Kate and I put in our new proposal for the Make a Difference Project.

"We believe in our project, Miss Jenkins. We are going to go ahead with it," I said.

"It sounds like a good idea but you will have to go to Mr. Rodriguez for his permission," said Miss Jenkins.

"I think you girls have a great idea. You will have to put in a request to the school board and get on their agenda before the end of May," said Mr. Rodriguez when Kate and I went to his office.

"Let's make more posters and get another petition together. That may help," said Kate.

"Great idea, Pickle. We should make some cookies and put a turtle sticker on each package. We'll give everyone who signs the petition one."

"Sounds like a smashing plan, Cabbage," Kate said.

"Paper is out-dated. If you want to show the school board how cool it is to have tablets and save trees, it will be best to have the kids sign my tablet. I'll set it up so you can use the stylus and store the signatures," said Elliot at Monday Night School.

"That is so cool, Elliot," Kate said.

Kate and I were at her house baking cookies for the petition signing.

"Elliot has a super-big crush on you, Kate. He blushes when he talks to you."

"No he doesn't. He is nerdy. I don't like him."

I saw her face turn red.

As we were taping up the posters in the eighth grade hallway, Steven Lancaster came over to put in his two-cents.

"What a lame idea. Why would you get rid of books? It is so easy to carry books," he said as he swung his bulging backpack over his shoulder. "Ouch," he screamed in pain.

"So heavy books are not a problem?" Kate asked.

"No I can handle them. I am strong," Steven said as he walked away rubbing his shoulder.

We set up the petition signing station in the lunchroom every day that week. Elliot's tablet came in handy. It was better than the stacks of paper we used for our first petition.

The tablet kept track of all the signatures. We didn't have to count them by hand. It seemed like we were finally going to succeed. Kids were stopping by, signing the petition, and enjoying the cookies.

Steven Lancaster walked by our table the next day at lunch. His arm was in a sling.

"Hey, Steven, how about signing our petition? We will give you a cookie," I said.

"No. I don't want a cookie," said Steven as he walked away.

"Wow, everyone's talking about your Make a

Difference project. It will be so cool to have a light backpack," said Kelsey. She had come up to our lunch table alone. "I'll sign your petition."

"Thanks. Here's a cookie," Kate said.

"What about Mallory? Do you think she will sign?" I asked.

"I'll send her over," said Kelsey.

Kelsey wasn't that bad when Mallory and her weren't together.

After all but two seventh-graders signed, on Friday right before lunch hour was over, Mallory came by and signed the petition. Steven walked over and signed with the arm that was not in the sling.

"Hey, where's my cookie?"

"Here it is," said Kate as she handed it to him.

"I don't know why I ever liked him," Kate said as Steven Lancaster walked away.

I smiled. "You like Elliot. Face it."

We got permission and a special hall pass from Mr. Rodriguez. I stood outside the door of the sixth grader's lunch period, then I gave the tablet to Kate and she stood outside the door of the eighth grade lunch period. We had all the signatures by the end of the third week of May.

"I got a letter from the school board. We're on their agenda for next Monday night," said Kate.

"Do you think the religious school principal will let us miss Monday Night School?"

"Sure my dad will let us miss," Kate said as we

both laughed.

Spring Concert finally came. Our families were in the audience. Kate and I were in the last number before the finale. We knew every word and harmony by heart. The last time we practiced we sounded like the contestants on American Idol.

We started to sing our duet. Kate opened her mouth. Nothing came out. Mr. Balbes started the music again.

I looked at Kate, she looked at me. We both started to laugh. Mr. Balbes looked so annoyed. I felt bad for letting him down.

He started the music one more time. Kate began to sing. I joined in at the appropriate time. We finished our song. The audience was applauding. Mr. Balbes smiled and gave us the thumbs up.

Last summer I would never have thought Kate and I would be able to sing a song together, let alone be friends. This was turning out to be a great school year. I was finally happy we moved.

The night came to present our idea. We organized as many kids as could to come with us. We held up our posters and paraded in front of the members of the school board.

Kids spoke about their back problems from carrying heavy books. Steven Lancaster showed them that his arm was still in a sling from throwing his heavy backpack over his shoulder.

At the end of our demonstration, the president of the school board said, "Miss Elkavich and Miss

Baker, this has been a very impressive production. We will have to weigh all the pros and cons concerning a change from text-books to electronic books. Tablets for all students may be cost-prohibitive. We will get back to you when we reach a decision"

As we left the Board of Education building, Kate said, "I think we'll pass the seventh grade."

"I think so, too," I said.

CHAPTER 10
SCHOOL'S OUT FOR SUMMER

"You girls are treading on thin ice," Miss Jenkins told The Cabbage and I. "You can still change your Make a Difference project and pass seventh grade."

"No. We feel strongly about the health and welfare of our fellow students. We're waiting for the board of education to give us their answer before summer vacation," said The Cabbage.

"Did you get any mail today?" I asked The Cabbage on our way to the mall.

"No news yet, Kate. I don't want to repeat seventh grade. I hope we hear something soon."

We were at the mall to buy new clothes for camp. After lunch we walked through a few stores. We were searching the latest arrivals for summer at our favorite shop.

"I have always wanted a top like this," said The Cabbage as she picked up a blue halter top.

"Me, too. You get that one and I'll get the pink one. We won't match exactly, but we will be like the twins at camp, Mandi and Amanda."

Tom Forrester, The Cabbage's uncle, and the director of Camp Anishinabe, had come to the stable over Memorial Day weekend to pick up King and take him back to camp. Summer vacation was almost here. We were going to have a blast!

With a few days left of school, the school board still hadn't sent us an answer. Our lack of a completed Make a Difference project was getting us an incomplete.

The weather was muggy. There was only one day left of school. Our school didn't have air conditioning. It was unbearably hot.

"Let's wear our new halter tops to school tomorrow," I said to The Cabbage.

"Are you kidding? We'll get in so much trouble, Kate. You know the dress-code says we must have our shoulders covered."

"I can't stand another day of sweating in the classrooms. I'm wearing my halter top tomorrow whether or not you wear yours."

The next morning as I left my house my mom said, "Kate, why are you wearing that big, heavy poncho? It is going to be so hot today."

"It's okay, Mom. I'm not hot at all."

I was swimming in sweat by the time I got to the Cabbage's house to catch the bus.

"I'm wearing my halter under here," I whispered.

"I am wearing my halter under my poncho, too," The Cabbage said as she lifted the heavy knitted material to show me she was wearing the forbidden garment, too.

We got off the bus and walked upstairs to our lockers. We took off our ponchos at the exact same time.

"Good luck, Pickle," said The Cabbage as she went down the hall toward her homeroom.

"You look great, Cabbage," I said as I went into

my algebra room.

"Young lady you know that halter top isn't allowed on the dress code."

"Mr. Kulis, I can wear whatever I want. It's the last day of school. It's almost summer vacation."

"I don't care. You still have to conform to the rules. You have to go to the office. Take the hall pass and go see Mrs. Brown."

Rules, schmules. School was all about rules. They told you what to wear, what time to eat and how many heavy books to carry.

The Cabbage was coming down the hall at the same time as me. When I opened the door we were greeted with a blast of frigid, polar air. We entered the air-conditioned office.

"Kate Baker and Jo Ann Elkavich to see Mrs. Brown." I said to the sweater-wearing secretary.

She ushered us into Mrs. Brown's private office.

"Girls, it looks like you didn't follow the school's rules. We have a dress code. You will have to cover up for the rest of the day. Do you have jackets in your lockers?" asked Mrs. Brown.

"I have a poncho," said The Cabbage.

"So do I. Why do you have air-conditioning in your office and not the rest of the school?"

Mrs. Brown didn't answer my question. She said, "Go to your lockers and put on your ponchos. You will have to wear them the rest of the day."

"But it's too hot. We will melt!" said The Cabbage.

"Then I'll call your parents to bring you suitable clothing."

"No. Don't bother. We'll wear our ponchos. It's only for a few more hours," I said. "After all, this is our last day of seventh-grade."

"Not exactly. I just received a list of the students who will be repeating the year and both of you girls are on the list."

"It isn't our fault we haven't heard from the board of education. Now we have earned an incomplete in social studies. And that's going to keep us from moving to the eighth-grade?"

"Don't be sarcastic. Yes, Miss Baker. It appears to be the case. I will see you in the fall. That will be all," said Mrs. Brown as she handed us each a hall pass and dismissed us from her office.

"At least we will be repeating the seventh grade together," The Cabbage said.

"Yes. And we'll be going to camp together this summer. That will be fun," I said.

"Kate, I know I promised you would go to Camp Anishinabe this summer, but Grandma fell, and this time she broke her hip," Mom said.

Last summer Grandma broke her pelvis falling off of a mechanical bull at a country music concert. Last week she broke her hip skate boarding. My grandma was always doing wild things.

"I just got off the phone with Aunt Elise. I told her we are going to come to Canada for the summer to take care of Grandma's house while she's in physical rehab. Someone has to tend her garden and watch her pets."

"No way, Mom. I'm all set to go to camp with Jo Ann. I can't believe you are going to ruin this for me."

"You and Timmy have to come with me. We'll be gone all summer. Dad will be in Israel with the eighth graders for the first two weeks. You won't have anyone to stay with before camp starts."

"I can stay with Jo Ann's family."

"No you can't. They're going to the U.P. to see their grandma before camp starts. You will go with me to Canada to spend time with your cousins. You'll have more fun in Canada than you ever did at camp."

"Mom. I never had fun at camp. Camp Anishinabe wasn't fun. It was punishment. I hated every minute. The camp has been remodeled. They have toilets that flush and beautiful new cabins. I'll be working in the stables with Jo Ann and I'll get to ride King again."

"Your cousin Nessa has horses. You can help her take care of them."

"At camp I'll be practicing to be a counselor in training. Camp is finally cool and you are not letting me go," I yelled.

"Kathryn, please don't raise your voice to me."

"How am I going to study for my Bat Mitzvah? Do you want me to do bad on it?"

"Badly, Kate," Mom corrected me.

"I don't even know my haftorah yet!" I tried

reasoning with Mom.

"You can practice while we're in Canada. If you have problems, you can Face Time with Dad."

"You mean Dad won't be coming up there after Israel?"

"He has to stay home after Israel. They need him to run the religious school at the temple. He will only be able to join us for the last two weeks. Then we'll all come back together and finish the preparations for your Bat Mitzvah.

I have all the centerpieces done and the party is planned to a "t". The responses are coming to my E-mail since I sent all the invitations out electronically to save on paper," Mom explained.

My mom could plan a big party three thousand miles away! I couldn't believe I was not going to camp. There was no way I could learn my Bat Mitzvah on my own. I was going to stink.

"No offense, Mom, but you aren't nearly as good a cook as Grandma. What will we eat there?"

"You don't look like you're starving. Nessa is only one and a half years older than you. Timmy has Danny and David to play with. Maurice will be home most of the summer. You'll have plenty to do. Don't worry so much. It will all work out."

"I am going to miss being at camp with you this summer, Cabbage."

"It won't be the same without you, Pickle. Try to stay out of trouble."

"It's too dull there to get into any trouble," I

said.

Dad loaded our suitcases in the minivan and off we went to the airport.

"I need to carry your passports since you are both minors." My mom walked ahead of me "And don't say anything. Let me do the talking."

Timmy went first. Amazingly, he didn't ask any embarrassing questions. The security guard let him through and had him wait for us on the other side of the rope.

"Hello, young lady. Where were you born?" the guard asked me.

"I was born in Michigan. Have any planes been hi-jacked lately?" I asked.

The guard said a code word into his radio on his shoulder, and before I knew it, I was being whisked away into a room at the back of the check-in area. The last thing I saw before I was surrounded by security agents and the door shut was my mom shaking her head.

"Young lady. Why would you ask such a question? You could ask, 'can I have a window seat?' or, 'is the plane on time?' You don't ask dangerous, controversial questions. We automatically have to check out any threats," the female guard said as she frisked me.

A male guard had dumped out my purse and my backpack and was going over everything with a special wand.

"Jack, she's clear," said the matron. Jack took a special stamp and with a lot of flare, he stamped my passport.

"Please, think before you speak. We could have stopped you from going to Canada. Have a nice trip," said the woman guard.

When I came out of the room, my mom and Timmy were sitting in chairs outside the door.

"Kate. Whatever moved you to say such a foolish thing?"

"I was curious. I'm so sorry, Mom."

"Wow, what did they do to you in there, Kate?," asked Timmy.

"Shut-up. Mind your own business."

When we got on the plane, I wasn't allowed to sit with Mom and Timmy. I had to sit by the window with an empty seat between me and a big, tough looking man.

He looked straight ahead the entire time we were in the air.

"Pardon me, sir. I need to use the restroom."

He stepped out into the aisle and followed me to the restroom. I noticed he had a holster with a gun inside his jacket.

"Why do you have a gun? Are you a terrorist?"

"I am a Sky Marshall. I have been assigned to keep an eye on you during the flight. If I were you, I would keep the questions to yourself."

He waited outside the door while I went to the bathroom. He then escorted me back to our seats where we sat silently for the rest of the flight.

When we got off the plane, my mom spoke to the Sky Marshall alone for a few minutes.

"Kate. You need to be more careful of what you say. You're lucky you didn't get into more serious trouble."

"I definitely will be more careful in the future, Mom."

We took a cab to the ferry boat. Timmy and I went to the gift shop to buy snacks. It was too windy to sit on the outside deck. There was nothing to do for two hours but look out the window at the ocean.

When we got off the ferry, we were greeted by Uncle Fred, Mom's younger brother. After a long, winding drive through the mountains, he dropped us off at Grandma's house. I could tell it was going to be a long, boring summer.

The rehabilitation center was across town. We drove there in Grandma's car. She was in the courtyard sitting in a wheelchair, drinking tea.

"Kate, it's good to see you. Your hair has grown long. I like it," said Grandma.

"Thanks, I finally can wear it in a pony tail."

"Sorry you didn't get to go to camp with Jo Ann."

"That's okay, Grandma," I said. It really wasn't okay. This was going to be the worst summer, ever.

I had to sleep on the sofa bed in the basement. It had an iron bar right in the middle that poked my back all night.

When I was seven, all the cousins were staying over at Grandma's and the beds were taken. The only place she could think of for me to sleep was in a blow-up swimming pool. It smelled like moldy rubber and I was hot and sweaty all night. Now I was stuck on the pull-out sofa.

The next morning I was rubbing my back while I came into the kitchen for breakfast. Uncle Fred and my mom were sitting at the table drinking coffee.

"Is your back sore?" asked my mom.

"Yes. It is sore. Can I sleep with you tonight, Mom?"

Cousin Nessa was at the table, too. I didn't know what to say to her. I was always shy with my cousins when I first saw them.

"You could sleep with me tonight, but you don't like my snoring," Mom said.

"Where's Timmy?" I asked.

"He got up early. Aunt Elise picked him up. He's staying at her house with cousins Danny and David for a few days."

"Get your stuff together. You're coming to my house," Nessa said.

"What about my mom? She may need my help in the garden."

"No, Kate. Come stay with me. My mom is away at University. We will have a great time at my house."

My suitcase wasn't totally unpacked so I went to my room in the basement and grabbed it. I was relieved not to spend another night on that uncomfortable pull-out couch.

Uncle Fred dropped us off on his way to work.

"No riding until I get home, girls."

"Okay, Dad," Nessa yelled as he drove away.

"Did you bring your boots, Kate?"

"They're in my suitcase. Your dad said not to go riding."

"He won't know. Let's go."

We went to the barn and saddled up Nessa's Arabians.

"When I used to ride in horse shows, I would take Duke. He's getting old so my dad bought me Aspen last summer. You can handle Duke."

"Sure, I rode at camp for four summers. My friend, Jo Ann, brought home a horse from camp and we got to share him this spring. We boarded him at a barn near our neighborhood."

"I heard about your trip to the air base. How do you get caught doing all these dumb things? You have to learn to out-smart your parents like me. My dad will never know we took the horses out," she said with a wink.

We rode down the mountain toward town and turned off of the main road and onto the trails. We were trotting at a nice pace. After about half-an-hour we got to a small lake. We wrapped the horses' bridles around some low tree branches.

"It's hot. Let's go swimming," said Nessa.

"I didn't bring my suit."

Nessa stripped down to her underwear and bra and jumped into the pond.

"C'mon in. The water's fine."

I looked around. There was no one in sight. I

took off my shorts and t-shirt and jumped in. The water felt refreshing. When we got tired of swimming, we lay in grass. Without towels, we used the sun to dry off.

We rode back to the house. In the kitchen there were two chocolate sundaes on the counter.

"My dad was here. He must have seen the horses were gone."

"Are we going to be in trouble?"

"You won't be in trouble. I might, though," said Nessa.

When Uncle Fred came home later that day, he said, "I don't mind you riding. Next time call me on my cell so I'll know where you went."

"Your dad is so nice. I would have been grounded."

"I am an only child. There's no one to tattle on me. If my dad grounds me, I'll just sneak out while he's at work," Nessa said.

The next two weeks, on week-days, we kept busy riding the horses to the lake when it was hot, and walking to town when it rained. On weekends, we stayed at Grandma's house with my mom and Timmy.

I was dreaming that I had fleas. I was itching like mad in my dream. I woke up with Baxter, Grandma's Bichon, laying on top of me, scratching like mad.

Nessa woke up scratching, too.

"Baxter, you nasty dog, get away," she yelled as she pushed the white, curly-haired pooch off the bed.

"Wow. Do you think we have fleas?"

"No. We feel itchy since Baxter was scratching," said Nessa. We both were rubbing our backs after climbing out of the pull-out couch bed.

The summer was dragging on and we were getting bored. Then, Nessa's mom, Aunt Patty, came home for a weekend.

Aunt Patty, Uncle Fred, Nessa, and I got into their camper early one morning, and drove for hours on narrow roads winding through the mountains.

Finally we got to Pachena Bay. Nessa and I pitched a tent on the beach while Aunt Patty and Uncle Fred set up the camper for themselves.

Nessa's parents let us go our own way. They weren't over-protective like my mom and dad. The two of us swam in the ocean and played on the beach all day.

"You want a piece of gum?" Nessa asked.

"Sure. Thanks." I couldn't believe I was chewing gum that wasn't sugarless. My mom never let me have regular gum.

"It would be cool to paddle across to explore those caves. I wish we had a canoe," I said.

"We could swim, but there is quite an under-tow in this area," Nessa said as we walked along the beach.

"Look, Nessa. There's a canoe," I pointed at an old, worn-out wooden vessel over-turned and partially submerged in the sand.

We dug around the canoe and eventually we were able to turn it over.

"I think it will make it across," said Nessa as she started dragging the beat-up canoe toward the inlet.

I grabbed the other end of the canoe and we set it into the water. We both climbed in. Nessa pulled out the oar that was stuck under the two benches.

"Let's take turns rowing," said Nessa.

Nessa rowed a few strokes, then I took over. We were about half-way across the inlet to the caves.

"We are taking on water," said Nessa. "There must be a hole in the bottom of the canoe."

I found the hole and Nessa and I combined our gum and tried to plug it. The water stopped for a few seconds, but the gum didn't hold for long. Water began rushing into the bottom of the canoe.

The vessel was filling up quickly with water. We began to sink.

I started paddling furiously, all the time trying to turn the canoe around to get back to shore. The canoe stubbornly wouldn't move. We were taking on more and more water and sinking faster.

"We have to jump out," yelled Nessa.

"I thought you said there was a dangerous under-tow!"

"Well, it's either sink or swim, and I am swimming," said Nessa as she dived out of the canoe and swam to shore. I followed suit and was not far behind as we trudged through the sand.

We sat breathlessly on the shore and watched as the last bit of the canoe sank into the water. Our plan of exploring the caves went under water with the canoe.

"What did you girls do with our canoe?" asked the shorter of two boys walking toward us.

The other boy, taller than his friend and with longer hair said, "You stole our canoe. You'll have to pay."

"We're not paying for that piece of junk. Besides, it had a hole in it. That old canoe couldn't even make it over to the caves," said Nessa.

"We were planning on repairing the canoe and using it ourselves. You should have left it alone. Who gets into a boat without checking for holes?" asked the shorter boy.

"Our day is ruined. What are we going to do now?" I asked.

"My dad isn't home. We can take his out-board and go across to the caves," said the taller boy.

"That sounds cool," said Nessa as she started walking off with the two boys.

"Hey, I want to talk to you," I said as I grabbed her arm and pulled her aside. The two boys stood a few feet away, waiting. "Do you know them?"

"We know them now. It will be fine. We'll have fun," Nessa whispered.

"We can't go with strangers to some caves. We should ask your parents."

"I thought you were cool," Nessa whispered to me. "Hey, guys, I forgot we have to go somewhere with our boyfriends. See ya later."

As we walked away, the tall guy said, "you owe us for the canoe."

"Yeah, right. Try to collect," yelled Nessa as we ran toward our campsite.

"Wow, that was a close call," I said.

"You are a baby, Kate. Now what are we going to do the rest of the day?"

Uncle Fred was at the campsite starting a fire to cook some fish he caught while we were gone. Aunt Patty was mixing up biscuits and already had corn on the cob, wrapped in foil, ready to put in the hot coals.

"Kate and I are tired of swimming. Can we go somewhere this afternoon?"

"Sure, Nessa. How about a drive after lunch?"

"Sounds great, Dad," Nessa said.

Everyone's stomach was full with the delicious lunch. We piled in the truck and drove along the curving road to a different beach.

"Are you ready to have fun, Katie?"

"Sure am, Uncle Fred," I said as we walked through a small grove of trees.

We came to a clearing. Along the shore there were cliffs with designs in the walls. We walked to the end of a cliff. It was at least twenty feet above the water.

"These are petroglyphs. They date back over two hundred years. The ancient First Nation tribes hung over the side by a rope and carved messages for other tribes in the sides of the cliffs. As they sailed by on their boats they knew which tribes were in the area and if they were friendly or not," Aunt Patty said.

The next thing I knew, Nessa dived off the edge of the cliff and into the water below.

"Come on in, the water is great," she yelled.

I took a leap of faith and jumped in. As we tread water we were able to clearly see the writing on the wall of the cliff. I wasn't sure if they were friendly, but the drawings were beautiful.

After playing in the water for a while, we swam to a small beach and hiked back through the trees to the parking area. Aunt Patty and Uncle Fred were waiting for us.

On the drive back to our campsite we stopped at a road-side stand and ate the most delicious French fries and fried halibut.

We spent the night in the tent using a flashlight to see as we played cards. Nessa was a bit bossy, but we did have fun most of the time.

I was concerned about her wanting to go off with strange boys. She was a bit of a 'free spirit' as my Mom once told me.

The Cabbage was more cautious than my cousin. I missed her. I wished I was at camp. There wasn't much I could do about it. I wasn't going to Camp Anishinabe this summer. I was stuck in Canada. I listened to the sound of the ocean washing up and down the sand. I soon fell sound asleep.

The next morning I unzipped the tent and

walked out on the sand. The tide was way out and up and down the beach there were hundreds of seals sprawled out in the sun. It was a sight to see!

We ate breakfast in the camper. Afterwards, Nessa and I folded up our tent. The four of us piled into the cab of the pick-up and headed out on the highway. The ocean was on our left as we drove toward the north.

There was court off the road where the land jutted out into the harbor. There were six small wooden houses lined up on the dirt road.

"It looks like these houses are abandoned," said Uncle Fred.

"Let's see what the people left behind," said Aunt Patty. "Sometimes you can find interesting artifacts."

"My mom is studying anthropology," explained Nessa.

"What's that?" I thought I heard of everything, but I never heard of anthropology.

"It is the study of man," said Uncle Fred as he led us into the first house. The door was open and there appeared to have been no one living there for a long time. There were clothes and boxes strewn all over the front room.

"Look, there's a baby bottle with sour milk in it," said Nessa.

"Ewww. That looks gross," I said.

"It seems like the people who lived here left in a hurry," said Aunt Patty.

"It may seem that way," I said, pointing out the

window, "but I think they're coming back."

There was a small boat with an out-board motor heading straight toward the little enclave of houses. The closer the boat got, the more apparent it seemed that we were going to be caught snooping through someone's house!

Nessa said to me, "Look, it's the boys from the beach!"

Sure enough, it was the tall boy and the shorter boy and a few of their family members. Before they docked their boat, the four of us ran out through the front door and jumped into Uncle Fred's truck. He started the motor and off we drove.

"That was a close one," said Aunt Patty.

"Mum, you have to be more careful with your field research," said Nessa.

"You can say that, again," I said.

We all laughed.

After driving a while, the ocean was no longer visible. We were winding through the mountains and came upon a huge lake.

"How about a swim?" asked Uncle Fred. "It is getting too warm."

We took turns going into the camper to put on our bathing suits. Nessa had a bottle of shampoo in her hand when we walked toward the water. The lake was crystal clear, but I couldn't see down to the bottom. We swam out quite far. There was a huge mountain on the other side of the lake.

We were treading water when Nessa dunked her head into the water to wet her hair. She squeezed out some shampoo into her hand and started lathering up her hair. I had never seen anyone wash their hair in a lake.

It looked so refreshing. I dunked my head and held out my hand. Nessa put some shampoo into my palm. I rubbed my hands together and started washing my hair.

We piled the foamy suds up on top of our heads and swam around for a while.

"Girls, time to come back," Aunt Patty was calling and signaling us to swim to shore. We swam under water to rinse the shampoo out of our hair.

"We have to head home," said Aunt Patty as she handed us each a towel to dry off.

"How did you like the bottomless lake, Kate?" asked Uncle Fred as we drove down the highway.

"Bottomless lake? I didn't know it was bottomless! How can it be bottomless?"

"They say the lake is two times as deep as the mountain is high. There have been many cars that have run off the road and never been found since there is no bottom to the lake," said Nessa.

Wow. There were a lot of fun things to do there. I guess it wasn't so bad to be in Canada instead of at camp.

CHAPTER 11
MAPLE LEAF MAGIC

Dad was on the phone when I got to Grandma's house.

"Have you been studying for your Bat Mitzvah?"

"Not exactly. I haven't had time. I've been so busy with Nessa. We're having a blast!"

"You have to prepare. It is already July. I'll be there in two weeks. We can go over everything when I get there. Practice makes perfect!"

I got the message, but I still didn't have time to practice. Nessa and I were having a great time hanging out. I loved staying at her house.

Her mom went back to the university and her dad was at work all day. My mom was busy helping Grandma since she had completed rehab and was back home. Her hip was healing well.

I hadn't seen my brother Timmy in days. It was cousin Danny's birthday. We were at Aunt Elise's house to celebrate. They lived at the top of a big hill on a gravel road.

Cousin Danny was one year younger than me and Cousin David was one year younger than Timmy. They had bikes of all sizes in their shed. Each of us grabbed a bike and lined up at the top of the hill for a race.

Nessa and I were the oldest cousins that day. Maurice was older than both of us, but he went with his parents on a trip to Alberta to visit his dad's family.

The three boys, Nessa and I, were at the top of the hill. Danny and David's dad, Uncle Sheldon, was there to yell," On your mark, Get set, Go!"

We barreled down the hill as fast as we could. Dust was billowing out behind our tires as the gravel crunched beneath them.

Suddenly, for no apparent reason, Timmy drove his bike in front of my bike. I thought I was going to hit him. To slow down I squeezed the hand brakes. Only the front brakes engaged.

Before I knew it, I was sailing over the handlebars and tumbling down the hill, somersaulting head-over-heels and heels-over-head until I came to an abrupt stop on the flat part of the road at the bottom of the hill.

I was wearing shorts and my pink halter-top, so there was no protection for my arms and legs. I was covered in dirt and sharp, hard pieces of gravel were embedded all over my body. The pain was numbing.

My brother and my cousins helped me to my feet. They guided me up the hill to the house. Every step I took sent excruciating messages of agony to my brain.

Uncle Sheldon picked me up and carried me into the house. He sat me on a kitchen chair and Aunt Elise started plucking each piece of gravel out of my skin with a tweezers. After she carefully cleaned and disinfected each wound, she dabbed on antibiotic cream with a cotton-tipped applicator.

"Wow, Kate. You're so brave. You aren't even crying," said Timmy.

That is when the floodgates opened. I started sobbing and couldn't stop. I was covered from head-to-toe with bandages. Every inch of my body hurt.

My mom had been quiet up until that moment. She came over and took me by the hand to the spare room. "Kate, take these pills for pain. I can't believe how mature you are becoming this summer. Lie down and rest."

"Mom. I don't want to miss Danny's party. Can you tell me when the cake is served? I want to be there to sing Happy Birthday."

"I'll come get you," said Mom.

I don't remember anything after that. When I woke up I was still in some pain. Aunt Elise's house was dark.

I walked slowly and carefully into the kitchen. I was starving. There was a night-light plugged into the back-splash. I noticed a plate covered in foil on the counter. There was a label placed on it with my name.

I took the plate to the table and got a glass of water from the bubbler next to the door wall. I sat in the chair and began eating. The food was delicious and the piece of birthday cake was fluffy and light. My aunt was a great cook.

"Hi, Kate. I thought I heard you. How are you feeling?" asked Aunt Elise.

"I'm better. I can't believe how fast I fell down the hill. My mom didn't wake me for the birthday."

"She tried to wake you. You were out for the count. You slept all night yesterday and all day today." Aunt Elise looked at the clock. "You slept about thirty hours. We felt you needed your sleep."

"I never slept that long before. That is amazing. I do feel a lot better. You did a great job patching me up."

I am a nurse, you know."

"I forgot. Why didn't you become a dental hygienist like my mom?" I asked.

"When we were girls, your mom and I went to Camp Anishinabe. My best friend at camp, Sharon, and I always wanted to become nurses. We even went to nursing school together."

"I didn't know that, Aunt Elise."

"Our mom sent us to camp in Michigan. That's where our Dad came from before he moved to Canada and met Grandma. He wanted us to experience Michigan. We loved camp. We made life-long friends with Sharon and Diane. Your mom and Diane were very happy when you and Jo Ann became friends."

"I wanted to go to camp all summer with her. Mom made me come here," I stopped when I saw the hurt look in my aunt's eyes. "I love it here, I really do. I was wrong about being bored. I am having a great time."

"I'm glad to hear that. Your mom went to stay at Grandma's. We'll take you there tomorrow. Go get some sleep," Aunt Elise walked me to my room. "Good night."

"Good night."

I lay in the bed. I thought I wouldn't be able to fall asleep since I had slept for thirty hours in a row. I closed my eyes. The next thing I knew, the sun was shining in the window.

When I got to Grandma's she was sitting at her kitchen table putting together a puzzle. I sat next to her and started fitting in pieces. The phone rang.

"How are you doing? That was quite a fall. You really got messed up," Nessa said.

"I'm better now."

"I called to tell you I am going to visit my mom at the university for the weekend. I'll see you when I get back."

I spent the next few days with my mom and Grandma. Timmy was still at Danny and David's house.

Mom and I drove Grandma to physical therapy and went shopping in town. We walked store-to-store and browsed.

"I wonder how Jo Ann is doing without me at camp? Do you think she misses me?" I asked as I paid for the dreamcatcher I was going to send to The Cabbage at camp.

"Yes, I am quite sure she misses you. Camp is not the same without your best friend," said Mom.

"I like my cousins, Mom, but I miss Jo Ann. As much as I hate the bugs at camp, I would like to be there right now. I want to see what it is like to sleep in the new cabin."

"Dad and I talked. He told me you're doing great on your Torah portion and after a few lessons with him you will have your Bat Mitzvah down-pat. After our family trip is over, he wants to send you and Timmy to camp for the last two weeks. When you get home, your birthday and Bat Mitzvah will come up fast.

I wrote a letter to The Cabbage at camp. I had already sealed her dreamcatcher in a big envelope, so I had the letter in a separate, smaller envelope.

There may have been new cabins and real bathrooms with flushing toilets at camp, but they still had snail mail and no internet. I wrote to The Cabbage and told her that I would be there soon. I mailed both things out from the post office in town.

Dad arrived at Grandma's house the next day. "It is great to see you, Dad," I said.

"I missed my little family," Dad said.

Nessa came back from University with her mom. Maurice and his parents returned from Alberta.

"We are going to have a regular family reunion for the next two weeks," said Grandma with a big smile.

Grandma waved at us from Aunt Patty and Uncle Fred's front porch. Maurice's mom and dad stayed behind to keep Grandma company.

"We are going to play euchre while you are

gone," said Grandma when she kissed me on the cheek.

Mom and Dad, Uncle Sheldon and Aunt Elise, Uncle Fred and Aunt Patty loaded into the front cab of Uncle Fred's truck. All six kids sat in the back bed of the truck.

Uncle Fred drove up the mountain slowly and carefully.

"Stay seated kids and hold onto the rail. We are going to go on some real steep, winding trails," said Uncle Sheldon through the back window of the truck's cab.

We reached a clearing, the truck stopped, and everyone piled out. Aunt Patty carried a picnic basket while Mom and Aunt Elise each grabbed an end of an enormous cooler, put it in the shade, and started a small camp.

The moms settled in to prepare lunch.

"We are going to go on an adventure today, kids," said Uncle Fred as he passed out sweaters to each of us kids. "Follow me." He was carrying a back-pack.

We walked toward some small hills. Dad and the Uncles led the way down a small hole in the ground with the cousins and I following. It got progressively darker as we slid down on our bums over the loose earth. Soon we were in total darkness. I couldn't see my hand in front of my face.

A light came on. Uncle Fred had a hard-hat on his head with a flashlight shining from the front.

The walls of the cave were illuminated. We were sitting on a ledge over-looking a small cavern. I had seen a similar cave on a National Geographic special on television.

Stalactites were hanging precariously over my head. I reached up to feel one of the sharp protrusions.

"Don't touch the formations, Kate," Uncle Fred said as the light on his helmet shined in my eyes.

"Sorry, Uncle Fred. I didn't know," I said.

"The caves are protected, but as a certified caver, my dad is allowed to take groups on guided tours," said Nessa.

"You know, Kate, there are bats in these caves and they love to nest in long hair," said Maurice as he reached behind me and ruffled my hair. I screamed. There was a loud echo.

They all laughed. I didn't think it was too funny.

"Every inch of stalactite and stalagmite takes about one hundred years to form. The stalactites hang from the ceiling and the stalagmites come from the ground-up."

He continued, "I have been caving for years and this is one of the most beautiful and accessible caves. Some caves have big pools of water and the formations are many meters tall. No one is allowed in those caves, since people got careless and were breaking off pieces of formations to keep as souvenirs."

He read my mind! I thought it would be cool to

bring a piece of the sparkly icicle formation home as a souvenir.

I felt like any minute a bat was going to creep into my hair. I jumped when cold drop of water dripped on my head. Uncle Fred finally stopped talking, and I was more than ready to go.

We climbed out of the cave and walked back to our picnic area. The cooler and baskets were there, but our moms were nowhere to be found.

"The ladies must have gone for a walk. They'll be back soon." said Uncle Sheldon.

We kids sat on some railroad ties and talked about bats and spiders. A good hour went by. We were getting bored and hungry.

"Where are our moms? Timmy asked with a worried look. He was like a baby sometimes.

Dad took his phone out of his pocket and dialed mom. "I have no bars. There is no cell reception this high on the mountain."

The cousins grouped together with our dads and spread out to look for our moms. We left pieces of ribbon tied to the trees so we would be able to find our way back. After an hour, we headed to the encampment.

"The kids are hungry. It's already three o'clock. We may as well eat lunch," said my dad.

"Good idea," said Uncle Sheldon.

Danny and David ran over to their dad.

"Do you think mom is okay? Where is she?" asked Danny. At nine years old, he was the youngest cousin. He started to cry.

"It's okay, Danny. Mum will be back soon. She can't get lost. She knows her way around," said David. At eleven, he was a year older than Timmy.

"I don't think my mom knows her way around. She gets lost going to the grocery store," I said. I was getting very worried. I started to cry.

"My mom knows her way around the mountain," said Nessa. She acted tough, but I could see she was concerned.

"Shel and I are going to drive down to town to call a search, said Uncle Fred after about two hours of waiting. Bruce, you stay here with the kids and wait in case the ladies return.

"What will we do if our mom's don't come back?" I asked Nessa.

"I don't want to find out!"

Uncle Fred and Uncle Shel came up the mountain with a line of trucks following them. Some of the men got out of their vehicles with dogs. Right away the dogs started to sniff the ground.

The search team was there to look for our moms. They organized everyone into groups and we set out on an official search.

At one point, dirt started swirling around our feet as a helicopter hovered over our heads. I covered my ears to block the noise of the propellers.

When the helicopter flew toward the other side of the mountain, I yelled my mom's name. "Debra Baker, where are you?" There was no yelling back in answer to my calls.

The sun was behind the peak of the mountain. All the searchers had returned to our original picnic area. It was getting dark. Our moms were still lost.

"There's not much more we can do tonight," said Uncle Fred. "We'll have to resume our search in the morning."

We quietly piled into the bed of the truck. All six cousins were so quiet, you could hear a pin drop. No one said a word. Tears were sliding down Nessa's cheeks. I felt pretty sad myself.

We drove down the hill in the darkness. As we approached Nessa's house, all the lights were on. I wondered if Grandma was okay.

The pick-up came to a stop on the unpaved driveway. The front screen door burst open and out came Aunt Patty, Aunt Elise and my mom! They were safe and sound.

I ran to my mom and hugged her harder than I had ever hugged her. Timmy was jumping for joy.

"My mom is okay. I am so happy," he yelled.

"We got a little turned around on the other side of the trestle," said Aunt Elise.

"When we got to the campsite you were all gone so we walked down the mountain and came home," said Aunt Patty.

"We're sorry for the confusion," said my mom. "We didn't know we were lost and you were looking for us!"

"You are all safe and sound," said Grandma, "I knew nothing would happen to my babies!"

The last week went by fast. The Canadian adventures had worn me out. The dreamcatcher was on the way to The Cabbage at camp. I couldn't wait to see her and tell her about my summer.

The final night at Grandma's house, with the bar on the pull-out couch digging into my back, I dreamt about The Cabbage's dad.

Mr. Elkavich had come back from the war. The Cabbage was sliding down a feather toward him. She was laughing as she landed in his arms.

I kept quiet and boarded the plane without incident. My parents, Timmy and I flew back to the States.

When we got home, I quickly packed my duffels for camp. I put in extra mosquito spray. I wasn't taking any chances. The Cabbage would be waiting and we were going to have a great time!

CHAPTER 12
CAMP STILL STINKS!

The new cabins at camp were great, but I liked the old tents better. It was more fun last summer with Kate, once we became best friends.

Aubra was seventeen and no longer a counselor-in-training. She was a full counselor and she had let it go to her head. She was constantly telling me what to do and bossing me around. I wrote Mom to ask if I could come home early and spend the rest of the summer at our house.

'No, Jo Ann', she wrote, 'I will be travelling a lot for work and you can't stay home alone. You are only thirteen. Besides, Aunt Sharon and Uncle Tom need more help than ever this summer.'

Since they had built the new cabins, the camp attendance doubled. My aunt and uncle couldn't find enough counselors to handle the new campers.

It was no use writing Mom back, even though I knew I would have no problem staying at home alone. As usual, Aunt Sharon and Uncle Tom assigned me to work in the stables to help with the horses. After having King all school year, I was tired of shoveling horse poop. The flies were driving me crazy.

The second week of camp I went into the main lodge to talk to my aunt and uncle.

"Can I have a different job this summer? I love riding the horses, but I want to sleep later and not get up at the crack of dawn to water and feed them."

"Jo Ann, you are great with the horses but we can get along without you. What would you like to help with this summer, instead of working in the stable?" asked Uncle Tom.

"Can I help with the rock wall and the zip line?"

"That will be fine, Jo Ann. We can use all the help we can get with those classes. They are very popular again this year," said Aunt Sharon.

The twins, Mandi and Amanda, came for second session. We had fun being in the new cabin, but it wasn't the same as the last summer when we were Mukwas. Being in the tent made us closer. In the large cabin, we shared a section with the older, fourteen-year-old girls from the Wakeshi Fox's.

"Remember last summer when we won the Talent Show? Kate was great at gymnastics," I said to the twins one morning at breakfast.

"All you talk about is Kate," said Mandi.

"You must really miss her," said Amanda finishing her sister's sentence.

They were right. Camp wasn't the same without my best friend. This was my sixth summer at Camp Anishinabe, and to be honest, I was tired of going to camp all summer.

The summer was dragging along. The only thing I looked forward to was when my mom came for visiting day every two weeks.

We would go to dinner at the Steak House in

town. After we ate we went for long drives in the country. Being with Aubra in the car for long periods drove me crazy.

If Kate was at camp, we would have gone to dinner with the Bakers and I wouldn't have had to hear how great of a counselor Aubra was, and how so many of the boy counselors were in love with her.

"Mom, can I come home with you? Please?" I begged when she was leaving.

"No, Jo Ann. I have to go out of town again. There isn't anyone to stay with you at home."

"Okay. I get it. I have to stay at camp."

When mom dropped me off from dinner, I went to the cabin. The bunk across from mine had a sleeping bag already stretched out on it. It looked like the sleeping bag Kate had last year. There were two duffels neatly tucked under the bunk.

Could Kate be at camp? I smiled at the thought and expected to see her walk into the room. Instead, to my disappointment, in walked Stacey Milgrim, The Pilgrim.

"Kate was supposed to be at camp all summer. At the last minute her grandma got hurt and she went to Canada," I said to Stacey as she climbed on her bunk to straighten her pillow.

"I am happy that brat isn't here," said Stacey. "I can't stand her."

"Hey. Kate is my best friend. You shouldn't talk about her that way. She isn't a brat!"

Stacey sighed, turned around, and stalked out

of the cabin. From that day on, she hung around with Norah, an older, new girl in the Wakeshi Fox's bunk.

The twins, Mandi and Amanda, took Stacey's side. For the next two weeks they didn't talk to me, and I didn't talk to them. Even though we had no more outhouses, camp really did stink!

"Jo Ann Elkavich," Aunt Sharon called my name during mail call on Friday.

She held up a large envelope. It was from Canada! Kate had sent me a care package decorated with orange markers, her favorite color.

We had an hour rest-period after lunch. I climbed up on my bunk. I remembered how much Kate hated the top bunk.

I opened my care-package. I pulled out something wrapped in tissue. I peeled back the paper. It was a beautiful dreamcatcher.

I looked inside the envelope. There was no letter from Kate. I wondered how her summer was going as I hung the dreamcatcher on the wall over my bed.

"What's that dumb-looking thing? It looks like junk," said The Pilgrim from her top bunk across the aisle from mine.

"It's special. It's a dreamcatcher. Kate sent it to me all the way from Canada."

"That's funny," said Stacey, The Pilgrim, Milgrim. "All the dreams you have will be nightmares if Kate sent it to you!"

"You don't know what a dreamcatcher does. It

stops the bad dreams from reaching you and only the good dreams can come in," I said. I couldn't believe I picked her as a friend over Kate last summer.

That night we had our last practice for the Saturday powwow. Third session would soon be over. The twins were leaving, but Stacey, The Pilgrim, would be staying for the last session.

There were only two more weeks left of camp. I couldn't wait. I was counting down the days until I would go home and could see my best friend, Kate.

I climbed into my sleeping bag. I looked back at the wall where my dreamcatcher was hanging. I hoped The Pilgrim was wrong. I didn't want to have a nightmare.

I was tired. I fell sound asleep. I dreamed that the man I saw out my bedroom window last fall didn't disappear in the fog.

I looked out my window. It was thundering and raining hard. The man rode up to the house on King. I flew down the stairs and opened the door. As I ran toward the horse, the sky lit up with a streak of lightening. It was raining so hard and the water filled my eyes. I couldn't see. I reached up toward the man. He pulled me onto the horse with him. As he hugged me close, the sun rose above us. We rode away on a rainbow.

My parents dropped me off on Sunday at Camp Anishinabe for the final session. Luckily, we arrived late and I didn't have to endure listening to the Forresters recite the Rules as I had all the previous summers.

"I can't wait to see the new cabin they built for us boys," said my little brother, Timmy as we walked through the playfield.

I was assigned to the Kokoko Owls, the bunk for thirteen year old girls. I was still twelve, but according to Sharon, the twelve year old bunk was full.

The new girls' bunk house was great. Flushing toilets in the bathroom, and real bunk-beds lined up in rows. The only empty bunk in our section was a top, but it looked like the bunk opposite it was The Cabbage's bunk. The dreamcatcher I sent her was hanging on the wall.

I had written to The Cabbage and was expecting her to be waiting for me. I was setting up my sleeping bag when in walked my arch enemy, The Pilgrim. She climbed up on The Cabbage's bunk.

"Why are you getting on Jo Ann's bunk? Where is she?" I asked.

"She left last night after the powwow. Her mom came and took her and Aubra home.

"Why is the dreamcatcher I sent her above your bunk?"

"Jo Ann said she hates you and didn't want that ugly thing, so she left it on the wall."

I felt tears sting my eyes. I couldn't believe it. "Why would she leave?"

"She said she can't stand you and went home

with her mom," said the Pilgrim as she jumped down from her bunk.

I stared at her in shock.

"Hey, Norah, this is Kate. She is only twelve. She is weird." Stacey, The Pilgrim, Milgrim, once my best friend at Camp Anishinabe, said as she walked away with the older girl.

Once again, The Cabbage failed me. She made me fail seventh grade, and now I was alone at camp. This was going to be a long two weeks.

CHAPTER 13
NO MITZVAH LIKE A BAT MITZVAH

My Bat Mitzvah going to be in a few days. Bubby and Zaide came in from Florida. The whole Baker's Dozen and their parents were staying at a hotel near the temple. Even the Canadian relatives were there.

"Kate are you excited?" asked Grandma as I walked by our guest room when she got in from Canada on Thursday night.

"Yes, Grandma I am excited about my Bat Mitzvah, but I am sad that I'll be back in the seventh grade."

"That is a bummer. At least you won't be alone. Jo Ann will be with you."

Grandma didn't know I wasn't talking to The Cabbage anymore. She was such a brat. When I sent her the dreamcatcher, I sent her a letter telling her I was coming to camp for the last session. She didn't have the decency to stay and wait for me. I had to put up with that mean Stacey, The Pilgrim, all by myself.

"Yes, and because of her we never finished our Make a Difference project."

"You gave it your best. I got you a new backpack."

"Thanks Grandma," I said as she handed me a cool looking, hand-painted backpack. I could imagine it weighed down with thirty pounds of textbooks.

"Look inside, Kate," said Grandma.

I pulled out an envelope. It must be a check for my birthday, I thought.

I tore it open without looking at the front. I pulled out the letter from inside. It was the letter I sent to The Cabbage at camp.

"The post office returned the letter. I thought you would like to have it back," said my grandma.

I felt my heart sink. I was so upset when I got to camp and found out The Cabbage left early. I thought she didn't care that I was coming to camp to be with her. The truth was, she didn't know I was coming to camp.

The next two days were filled with lunches and dinners with my out-of-town guests. When Saturday morning came, I was happy to finally get to my big day.

"I can't believe the Elkavich family isn't going to be here for your special day. In her text Diane said she will explain later," Mom said as we were getting in the car to go to the temple.

The rabbi called me up to the bimah to lead the congregation in the Sabbath prayers. All the practicing I did came in handy. I only made a few mistakes with the English. I did better with the Hebrew.

Different groups of relatives honored me with aliyahs. The blessings by my grandparents were especially sweet. Grandma walked up the stairs with Bubby and Zayde. You wouldn't guess she had a broken hip two months before.

My aunts and uncles came up for the second Aliyah. All twelve of them crowded around me. After the blessings it took so long for them to kiss and hug me, the audience started to laugh.

Mom and Dad came up with Timmy for the last aliyah.

"Kate, as principal of the Religious School, I have been on this bimah many times for Bar and Bat Mitzvahs. They have all been special to me. Never before has a B'nai Mitzvah been as special as today.

You are a fine young woman. You have amazed your mom and I with your maturity in the last few months. We are proud of you and know that with your spunk and determination you will accomplish all your dreams."

After the ceremony the entire congregation joined with my relatives and I for lunch in the social hall.

Saturday night the whole family got dressed in their fanciest dresses and suits. My party was in the hotel ballroom where the relatives were staying. Many kids from school were there.

The theme of my Bat Mitzvah was horses. Mom had finished the decorations and on the tables were the huge, colorful centerpieces she made last spring. I was lucky that she was the most organized lady!

Each table had a large horse with a cut-out figure of me on his back. There were bowls of candy and nuts and mints with my name written in orange icing. Bouquets of orange and white balloons were floating in every corner of the room.

After dinner the disc jockey called me up to a table with a huge cake. For each of my thirteen birthday candles I read the poems I had written for the different groups of people.

First I had a candle to remember my grandpa who passed away when I was little. Then I called my aunts, uncles and cousins. After they sat down all the boys at the party came up.

The boys came up in one large group to light a candle. Steven Lancaster pushed Elliot out of the way to stand next to me. He had a lot of nerve, acting like he was my close friend.

"Steven, would you mind stepping aside so Elliot can stand here?"

Elliot took his place next to me and put his hand on mine as I lit the candle. The photographer had everyone smile and took a picture.

"You are a good friend," I said quietly to Elliot before he walked back to his seat.

"You too," said Elliot.

The next candle was for all the girls at the party. Susan and Emily came up with a bunch of girls from school and temple.

"And now for Candle Number twelve, The Best Friend Candle, we call, Jo Ann Elkavich," announced the D.J.

I waved my arms at him and said into my microphone, "She's not here."

"I am here," said The Cabbage as she walked

toward the candle-lighting table and stood next to me.

"I couldn't miss your Bat Mitzvah. We just got back from our trip. I have so much to tell you," she whispered as we lit the candle together and smiled for the photographer.

The Cabbage walked away. I noticed her mom and Aubra standing next to a familiar looking, tall stranger.

The disc jockey announced the thirteenth candle and called Mom, Dad and Timmy.

After we lit the candle everyone sang Happy Birthday to me. It was the best birthday I had ever celebrated.

We walked over to my mom and dad's table.

"This is my dad. Dad, this is Kate Baker," The Cabbage said introducing me.

"Pleased to meet you, Mr. Elkavich."

"Nice meeting you, Kate," he said as we shook hands.

The Cabbage and I went toward the dance floor.

"That's why I wasn't at camp when you got there. My aunt and uncle didn't even know why mom picked up Aubra and I early. Dad was alive all these years. He was an under-cover spy in Afghanistan."

"Wow. I thought you ditched me."

"I didn't know you were coming to camp. By the way, thanks for the dreamcatcher."

I did send you a letter. Apparently, it got lost in

the mail."

"That's okay. Anyway, my mom came to pick us up at camp as soon as she found out Dad was alive. He couldn't let us know until the President gave him a security clearance. All those times we thought we saw him, it was him! "

The rest of the evening was spent dancing and playing contests. All year when I wanted Steven to be my boyfriend, he had no interest. Now, when it was too late, he was following me around and trying to dance with me.

"Time for the Hora. We need the Bat Mitzvah girl out on the dance floor," said the D. J.

Everyone came on the dance floor when the music began to play.

'Hava na gila, Hava na gila,'

People formed a huge circle and everyone joined hands. I was in the middle.

The crowd danced in a circle while different groups of people danced in the center with me.

Mom, Dad and Timmy were with me when the people in the circle raised their arms and smooshed in on us.

My Canadian cousins came to the center of the circle to dance with me.

Nessa said, "This is the best party I have ever been to. I wish I was Jewish!"

Toward the end of the song my uncles from both sides of the family brought a chair for me to sit on. They lifted me into the air and danced around. I was high in the air and held on tight so I wouldn't plummet to the floor. They brought more chairs and lifted my parents and of course, Timmy.

The D.J. called the kids to the floor for the final dance. It was a slow song. I looked for Elliot.

He was talking to The Cabbage. I walked over and put my arms around both of them. The truth was, this year I had been lucky enough to have two best friends. The three of us walked out to the middle of the floor and had the last dance together.

On Sunday morning my parents, Timmy and I met the relatives at the hotel for brunch. Dad drove groups of out-of-towners back and forth to the airport all day. We said our goodbyes at the hotel.

"Grandma, I thought you were going to stay longer. Why are you leaving?"

"Well, Kate, now that my hip is healed I have many chores to catch up on and I am starting my country dance lessons. I'll see you next summer."

Once again, Mom waited until the last minute to take us school shopping. It was Labor Day but we were too tired from the Bat Mitzvah weekend to celebrate. Dad was at the temple and Timmy was with us. He was his usual, annoying self.

"Mom can I get these shoes? Everyone will be wearing them," I said pointing to some glittery, flats.

"Kate, they are way too expensive."

"Please, Mom?"

"You won't throw them out?"

"No, I promise I won't."

How did she know I threw my shoes out last year? My mom did have eyes in the back of her head!

Tuesday morning I was sitting at the kitchen table dressed and ready to start the seventh grade again. The sooner I got there, the sooner it was going to be over with. School was really going to stink this year.

The doorbell rang at six o'clock. No one was downstairs yet so I went to the door and peeked out the peep-hole. There was a Unified Parcel Service truck in our driveway.

"Special delivery for Miss Kate Baker," said the uniformed man as he handed me a large white cardboard envelope.

"Please sign here," he said as he held the electronic signature box while I signed my name in the little square with the stylus.

I had been getting envelopes and packages all week with gifts for my Bat Mitzvah. I was about to add this one to the mail pile on the foyer table when I noticed the return address. Written across the front of the envelope it said:

Board of Education
Urgent Meeting Notification
Open Immediately

I tore open the envelope and read the letter out-loud.

"Dear Miss Baker, an emergency meeting of the Board of Education will be held today at seven-thirty in the morning. Your attendance is mandatory."

"Mom, Dad," I yelled as I knocked on their bedroom door.

Dad opened the door. He had shaving cream on his face and a clean track of where his five-o'clock shadow had been removed by the razor.

"Kate what's the problem? Are you okay?"

"Dad, look at this letter. You can't go to work. You have to take me to this meeting. They have made a ruling and have requested my presence."

"Debbie. Change of plans. Get Timmy ready. We are all going with Kate to the Board of Education meeting."

The phone rang.

"Hello?"

"Kate. Did you get a letter? Are you going to the meeting?" asked The Cabbage.

"Yes. I'll meet you there."

When we got to the Board of Education building, the parking lot was full. Dad had to circle around a few times and he ended up parking on the grass.

The Cabbage was waiting outside for me.

"Aubra and my parents are inside saving seats for your family. Let's walk in together."

We pushed through the doors at the same time.

The large meeting room was filled to capacity. Since all the seats were filled, there were people standing along the walls. We made our way down the center aisle. Everyone stood up and was staring at us.

Mrs. Cohen was there with Bryan and Ryan.

"There are our babysitters," said little Ryan.

Mrs. Cohen smiled and said, "Way to go, girls."

I wasn't sure what she meant.

As we walked further down the aisle I noticed many of our classmates were standing in the rows in front of their seats.

Miss Jenkins was on the end of one of the rows. Elliot Einstein and his mom were next to her. On the other side of the aisle, Mallory and Kelsey were staring at us.

"What are they doing here?" asked The Cabbage.

"I don't know, but look! There are Mr. Rodriguez and Mrs. Brown."

"Do you think we're in more trouble?" The Cabbage looked worried.

We were ushered to the lectern facing the Board of Education members. This wasn't a lucky spot for us back in May when our idea for the tablets was shot down by these very same people. Since then, we had gotten big, fat, incompletes in Social Studies and didn't pass the seventh grade.

How embarrassing it was going to be to repeat the seventh grade. Like Grandma said, at least I wouldn't be alone, The Cabbage would be there with me.

I whispered to her, "Why do you think we are here?"

"I don't know, Kate. The letter didn't say. Can you believe all these people showed up?"

The president of the school board smacked the gavel loudly on his desk and said, "Order. This meeting is now in order. Please take your seats and be quiet."

Everyone sat down. The room fell silent.

"Yesterday this esteemed board came down with a final ruling on the issue of heavy backpacks for our students.

Textbooks have always been a way of life for the students of this, and all areas, of our state. Over the summer we took the issue to the State Board of Education. Late last night they came up with a resolution.

"Kate Baker and Jo Ann Elkavich, you have certainly 'Made a Difference.' The State Board of Education is going to use our school system as a pilot. It will be called the Turtle Initiative after the wonderful idea you presented to this Board last spring.

Every student at East and West Hills Middle Schools and Lincoln High School will be receiving an electronic tablet loaded with his or her textbooks starting today, the first day of school."

The crowd cheered. The sound was deafening. The cheer team from Lincoln High was chanting, "No More Backaches, No More Backaches!"

The school board president banged his gavel and once again the room went silent.

"Do you girls have anything to say?"

"Just one thing. Are we passed into the eighth grade?" asked The Cabbage.

"Yes, Miss Elkavich. You and Miss Baker are now officially eighth-graders at West Hills Middle School."

The Cabbage and I high-fived each other as a photographer from the local newspaper took our picture.

The crowd cheered again. We were heroes. As we walked out of the room I started noticing more of our classmates and a lot of kids I didn't recognize.

Just as I realized the strange kids were from East Hills Middle School, Susan and Emily came up and hugged The Cabbage and I.

"You are famous! And we won't have back pain from carrying heavy books!" said Susan.

Emily said, "There is our ride. We have to get to East Hills before the first bell."

The Cabbage and I waved at them as they drove away.

Mr. and Mrs. Elkavich and Aubra pulled up in their van. Little Motown, their dog, was looking at me from the window.

"See you at school," said The Cabbage as she got in the back seat. The door shut and her mini-van drove away.

"Yes," I said to myself as I waved to her. "See

you at school, best friend."

ACKNOWLEDGEMENTS

My husband, David, and son, Michael, were understanding and supportive during the two and a half years it took to write School Stinks!

Kelly, my daughter, was a helpful editor.

My second son Joseph had little time to help with School Stinks! He was busy creating his own family and giving us our first grandson, Elliot.

Claire Epstein, my closest friend, listened to passages from the book and gave constructive criticism.

Kathie Allen and Alecia Holland, lent their expertise as proofreaders and cheerleaders.

Loyal readers of Camp Stinks! encouraged me to complete School Stinks! so they could see what Kate and Jo Ann were up to.

My good friend, Ray Dembek, lent his technical talent when I was in cyber-limbo.

Thanks to my late parents, Jack and Sylvia Blum, for giving me a chance to explore the world as a child. They were not over-protective and told me I could accomplish anything I put my mind to. I wish my parents were alive to read my books. They would have been proud to see their Pumpkin become an author.

ABOUT THE AUTHOR

In Camp Stinks! Karen Dawn Blum introduced readers to Kate Baker and friends.

School Stinks! gives voice to The Cabbage, Kate's on-again, off-again best friend.

Karen lives in Michigan within a few miles of her junior high. She works full-time as a hygienist in her husband's dental office.

Karen loves to bring people together. She enjoys planning parties and reunions for family and friends.

Visit Karen's website at
http://www.KarenBlumBooks.com.

Karen welcomes your comments via E-mail.
Karen@KarenBlumBooks.com.